Mary Layfield Mail Order Bride

Hannah Winstone

Published by Trellis Publishing, 2021.

This is a work of fiction. Similarities to real people, places, or events are entirely coincidental.

MARY LAYFIELD MAIL ORDER BRIDE

First edition. July 12, 2021.

Copyright © 2021 Hannah Winstone.

ISBN: 979-8224417711

Written by Hannah Winstone.

MARY LAYFIELD, MAIL ORDER BRIDE

HANNAH WINSTONE

MARY LAYFIELD, MAIL ORDER BRIDE

Mary Layfield departed the train at a quarter-past six in the evening, and by then the sun had already began to dip low over the horizon. Rich pink and orange spread across the town, drenching it in warmth. It was *beautiful.*

Mary liked to think it was a sign from God that this new beginning of hers was off to a good start. She hoisted her bags into slender but strong arms and stepped out into the street. The evening breeze hit immediately but it was gentle, refreshing with the warmth of the setting sun splashed across her face.

If Louisiana was like this all the time, Mary was going to love it here; although in all honesty, anything was better than the cramped, dirty and stuffy conditions back home. It was, after all, why she had left her home and family behind to marry a man here. Now, speaking of her fiancee- where *was* he? He had promised to meet her outside of the train station with a coach...

"Why *good evening,* who do we have here? I don't believe I've seen you around before."

Mary flinched at the voice and spun; but strands of thick black hair flew in her face and obscured her vision. With a huff of irritation she flicked her hair away - she *knew* she should have worn it in a tighter pin - only to be faced with a tall, slender man in a grey suit. Not her husband to be, and certainly not anyone she wanted to be bothered with. "I'm sorry sir, I'm just waiting on someone."

"I could always wait with you - I'd *hate* for someone as pretty as yourself to be picked up by an *unsavoury sort.*" He grinned - but it wasn't pleasant. He might have had a young, innocent face and a mop of blond hair, but that leering grin made Mary shudder. "It's unsafe for a young woman to be alone after dark."

She was *perfectly* capable of looking after herself, but Mary pinched her lips closed. Perhaps if she ignored him-

"The quiet type? I can respect that."

Moments passed - stretching on and on. Mary waited by the roadside, gaze flickering past the face of each man she saw. None were her fiancee. She was all too aware of the tall man inching closer and she shuffled away, using her suitcase as a blockade between them.

After a while he said, "I don't think this person you're waiting on is coming. Why don't you come with me instead? We could have so much fun-"

"I don't think so," she snapped, "I shall wait here a while longer."

"You're wasting your time, lady - come with me, I can show you a good time-"

A coach rumbled past, led by two enormous grey horses. It rolled to a stop, blocking out the rusty setting sun. A moment later a head poked out. "Ma'am, is this man causing you trouble?"

With a huff Mary approached the man in the coach. She saw a flash of metal - a Sheriff's badge - and heaved a sigh of relief. "He is - he's been harassing me for the last ten minutes and I'm becoming quite fed up."

The Sheriff hummed, "Well ma'am, I'm Sheriff Woolford, and I'm happy to help. If you're new in town you won't know that some of the men around these parts are *quite* uncultured. I would offer you a ride, but I'm on the way to the jail right now."

"That's absolutely fine," Mary replied with a sweet smile, "you can let me off outside and I'll be on my way. Please, I won't be a bother." She hefted up her bags - a pitiful amount, really, but almost everything she had ever owned - and stepped forward.

Behind her the tall man grunted, "excuse me, but I was simply offering this woman my company as she waited. How *dare* you suggest-"

"With all due respect *sir,* you've been rude and inappropriate the entire time."

His mouth hung agape, eyes slowly narrowing into a scowl. Somehow it suited him far more than that false smile he had worn only moments ago. Perhaps it was his *true* self shining through.

With a satisfied smirk Mary turned back to the Sheriff. "Please, allow me to ride with you just for a short while."

"The Sheriff's office - and the jail - is at the other end of town. I have a man with me, a man I've just arrested not forty minutes ago-"

"Is he dangerous?"

"No, just a thief."

"Then I'm sure I will be perfectly all right, especially with a Sheriff there to protect me."

The Sheriff sighed so deeply, like she was causing him the worst trouble in the world - but then the coach door swung open to reveal a simply furnished interior. He was silent as he helped Mary with her bags, and then offered an arm to assist her inside.

It wasn't until Mary sat down that she noticed the second man. He was broad shouldered and grizzled - but the bright gold of his hair offset that dark, brooding look. Actually, he was rather handsome. At least he was, until Mary realised he must have been the man the Sheriff arrested.

Mary had no chance to speak as the coach lurched into motion. She jerked forward, one arm thrown out to support herself - but a rough hand shot out to steady her before she fell. Her eyes met dark blue ones, and then travelled down to a broad, smirking mouth. With a gasp she snatched her arm back, back shooting straight. *"Don't* touch me!" She sounded like a mother scolding a child.

"I was only trying to help," he muttered with a roll of his eyes.

"Rex Sunderland, you keep your filthy hands off this lovely young woman."

That warning was enough for the man - *criminal* - to keep quiet. Even so he glared at the Sheriff with dark, deep set eyes. It was then that Mary realised he looked familiar; like the echo of someone she had seen before. Older, and considerably less refined but that golden hair, the unusual height. Well, it didn't matter. As soon as they reached the Sheriff's office she would never encounter him again anyway.

Silence descended upon the cramped stagecoach. Every bump in the road caused Mary to jump, elbow knocking awkwardly against the door. Although it was pleasantly cool outside the interior was stuff, the air thick and tense. She couldn't wait for the journey to end.

To keep herself occupied Mary turned her gaze to the tiny window. Outside the town rolled past - tiny houses all packed in together, narrow roads and equally cramped paths slowly spread out, interspersed with tall trees and lush green parks. The houses slowly faded out until all that remained were fields.

"I thought we were going to the Sheriff's office?"

Sheriff Woolford let out a laugh - it was sweet and cheerful. "Just taking a shortcut. It's easier to take the country roads than the weave through town. Only a few minutes longer."

"Seems to me like I've been stuck in here for hours," Rex muttered - but he dropped his head and scowled when Sheriff Woolford shot him a warning look.

Mary squinted over at him, lips pursed. She *knew* that face - but from where? It had been nagging at her since she sat down; and as much as she wanted to, she couldn't put it out of her mind.

There was no time to think about it as she lurched forward with a gasp. The coach shuddered as if rocking on its wheels, the force of it throwing Mary forward and into the seat across.

Beside her Rex also let out a muffled gasp, fists gripping the seats. "What was *that?*"

"Nothing to worry about," Sheriff Woolford assured - though his voice wavered, "these old roads can get bumpy sometimes, especially in the dark. No need to worry." Mary didn't like his tone of voice - nor the way he chewed his lower lip in worry.

"Taking shortcuts, as you put it, at the risk of our safety hardly seems responsible."

"I *assure* you, ma'am, that is not-"

He was cut off as the coach shook once more and it lurched to the side so ferociously Mary felt it tilt. The right wheels left the ground for a split second and the horses whinnied outside. There was a split second where she felt it settle and she sighed in relief - and then the wheels skidded, the coach grasping for purchase on the rocky ground. It shifted, swayed - and then the entire coach careened.

Mary threw out her hands to keep balance but it was too late - the coach was spinning madly and she was *thrown* against the door - the door that swung open with the force and she tumbled out with a shriek, heart thundering in her chest as she grabbed blindly for something - *anything* - to hold onto. Then her back impacted the cold, hard ground and pain shot through her shoulder. For a moment all Mary saw was blackness.

It subsided slowly and her vision swam back into view. Heaving herself up took every ounce of effort and she winced as heat laced its way along her left shoulder. How badly had she hurt herself?

There was no time to think as she sprang to her feet, eyes searching the darkness for the others. The Sheriff, the coachman, Rex... even if he was appalling, he didn't deserve to be *hurt*. Her head snapped from left to right, eyes straining to see - and there it was. In a ditch by an empty field. The horses seemed fine, loose from the coach but walking just fine.

Her ankle ached as she shuffled over. She had been thrown *so far* - or had the coach fallen all the way over there after she had been ejected from it? She shivered despite the nice evening.

"Shit."

The voice startled a gasp from her and she skittered back - and then Rex appeared from the other side of the coach. A deep scowl creased his features as he hoisted himself through the door - which now faced up to the sky as the coach lay lifeless on one side.

"Are you all right?" she called over.

"Fine."

"What about the Sheriff and coachman?"

"Who cares?"

It was Mary's turn to scowl, her usually dainty features furrowing. How could he *say* something like that? What kind of cruel, disgusting man-

Mary was snapped out of her thoughts as a hand gripped her slender arm and she grimaced at the dull ache settling there. When she glanced up it was right into the dark, misty blue of Rex's eyes.

"What are you doing?"

"Getting out of here."

"And why do you need me? We should get help; those two men might need medical care, or-"

Rex huffed, and eve in in the dark she saw the roll of those pristine blue eyes. "If we get help, then I go to jail. If I *leave,* I'm a free man." He tugged her once again, firmer this time, but not enough to make her move. He could if he wanted to - with that stocky build and the force of his grasp, there was no doubt about it.

Even so, she didn't allow herself to be intimidated. Standing tall, eyes meeting his she asked, "and why do you need me?"

"Leverage," was his only reply.

"Great," she muttered quietly, "I'm supposed to meet my fiance today, and instead I get stuck with a criminal." Mother did always say she had terrible luck.

"Excuse me?" Rex's voice softened, edged with confusion as he quirked a brow her way. His grip loosened, just a little, as he stared at her. "Your fiance?"

"Yes. Not that it's *any* of you business, but I travelled from Ohio-"

His eyes widened and he snatched his arm away as if he had been burned. "This is *impossible.* You're Mary Layfield?"

"I am."

"I'm your fiance."

Impossible. Mary knew her fiance was a man named Rex - but he had never informed her of his surname. It hadn't mattered, he said, not when they were going to have so much time to get to know each other. Now here he was, right in front of her and he was a *criminal.* Sh stumbled back, mouth agape.

Behind them a man grunted and the broken carriage door creaked.

"That's the Sheriff. Good to know he's alive." Rex grunted - and once again that strong hand gripped her painfully. "We'll have plenty of time to discuss this later - but we need to leave. I'm not going to jail."

Mary was helpless to refuse as she was propelled forward by a hard shove. She stumbled over hard ground but he caught her - and even that tough made her shudder. She just had time to crane her neck around to see the Sheriff climb out of the wreckage before they disappeared from view.

————————————————

Mary couldn't place how long they walked abut as time drew on her legs began to ache and the persistent pain in her shoulder progressed from a nuisance to a deep, uncomfortable cramp. It was silent too - so silent she felt even the clack of her boots was too much.

She kept her head down, fidgeting with the thick fabric of her shawl as they moved through town. She hadn't even noticed they had stopped until Rex left her side. A moment later light flooded the pavement and her gaze snapped up. He was holding a door open for her? A moment later she looked up - they were outside an inn.

"Hurry up, it's cold."

She did as he said, hurrying inside with a nod. Warmth hit her immediately and a relieved sigh slipped from her lips. After walking for so long it was *wonderful* to feel warmth hit her skin. The inn itself was simple and bare - with a seating area and a small fire blazing in the corner. Narrow stairs led to the rooms on the next floor.

A young man greeted them with a tired smile. "Good evening. Or night now, I suppose. What can I do for you?"

"Two rooms," Rex replied, "next to each other."

The innkeeper blinked but nodded. "Of course, sir."

Mary didn't hear the rest as she turned, slipping away to ease up to the fire. It crackled merrily as she sat down across from it, and she didn't hesitate to reach over and soak up that warmth. She could have happily stayed there all evening, just enjoying that heat and the gentle crackle of wood.

A shadow fell over, and she knew that was all the time she had to enjoy herself. Uneasiness settled in her stomach and she prepared for the worst - she knew so little of Rex, how was she to know what he thought or what he was going to do?

He simply collapsed down beside her. The old sofa creaked under his added weight and he grunted, shifting to put as much space between them as possible. Even so, it wasn't enough for her. He parted his lips as if to speak - and in the light Mary noticed a dusting of stubble for the first time - and then said, "I'm not some terrible, evil criminal you know."

She turned, brow raised. Something simmered under her skin but she pushed it down. "Oh? Then what were you doing getting yourself *arrested?*"

"I only stole from someone who deserved it," he answered gruffly, "so you can stop being so pretentious." He folded his arms - but there was something oddly defensive about it. He looked like a child having a tantrum, but there was something else too. He was *embarrassed.*

The revelation didn't make her feel any better. With a quiet hum of disapproval, Mary turned away. "You say that but you have no proof. How does *anyone* deserve to be stolen from? I see the clothes you wear and I can't see you were in need of money."

He was on his feet in a flash, so quick she didn't even see him rise. He loomed above her with a scowl, face obscured by dancing shadows from the fire. "I wouldn't expect *you* to understand. You don't know me, despite all of those letters we wrote to each other. You're just an arrogant, scornful woman."

"You're rude and terribly tempered," she replied evenly, "so you have *no* room to be frustrated. Remember you're the one to basically kidnap me."

"You would be stuck with me anyway, since we're to be married."

If the thought that was still going to happen, Rex was so incredibly wrong. He was going to get caught - first for thieving and now for carrying a hostage - and she was going to forget about him. What she was going to do all the way in Louisiana with no way home was another matter.

"Perhaps," Mary suggested, "we should sleep. We can argue more tomorrow - but don't think this conversation is over, and don't think I will be cooperative."

"I don't believe you know the meaning of the word," Rex snapped back.

Her eyes narrowed, lips pursed as she rose to her feet. Even if she barely reached his shoulder she glared up at him with *venom*, breathing even despite the way her chest lurched. "You're the one in the wrong, *Rex,* not me."

He looked as if he wanted to speak - but his shoulders slouched and he stepped back - allowing Mary space to leave. In that moment the fight had drained from him and he just looked *exhausted*. Under normal conditions Mary would have felt a pang of sympathy; but not for him.

She ascended the stairs without another word - and even though a small part of her wished to glance back she kept her gaze firmly ahead.

Something told her she wasn't going to sleep much tonight.

———————————

It took hours of waiting and listening - of pacing the narrow room and waiting for the perfect chance. That chance came at six o'clock in the morning. The bustle of the morning would arrive soon, allowing Mary's disappearance to go unnoticed for a time; and by the time Rex thought to wake her, she would be gone.

Mary crept quietly from her room, feet light on the ancient wooden floor. She cast a nervous glance to the room beside - where Rex slept - before making her way downstairs. She took each step with precision, slow and careful; and it wasn't until her foot hit the thick carpet on the floor below that she let herself breathe. Then she wrapped her shawl tightly around narrow shoulders and slipped outside.

The cold hit her immediately, wind hitting her face. Strands of dark hair flew into her eyes and brushing it aside only made more hair obscure her vision. She wrestled with it, wishing she had more pins to secure it in place - but she had left her bags with the upturned coach.

When she finally tamed that wild brunette hair she looked up - right into a pair of bright blue eyes. It was that man *again*.

"Ah, who would have thought we would cross paths again! I do hope you found that person you were waiting on." His smile, so cheerful and sweet, made her skin crawl. "What are you doing in a run down inn like this?"

"That's none of your business," she replied with a huff, "now if you don't mind, I have places to be."

"Where could that be? I'd be honoured to walk with you - I hate to think of a lovely woman like you walking alone so early."

Her eyes flickered up, lips parting to tell him *absolutely not* - but then she caught movement behind him. A man, tall and slender, wearing the uniform of a Deputy Sheriff. He stood across the road with a cigar stuck between his lips, watching them through narrowed eyes. Her heart skipped, relief settling in her chest - if anyone could help her, it was the Deputy.

It would have been so *easy* to alert the Deputy to Rex's whereabouts, to tell him everything and watch as Rex was taken to jail. Yet she hesitated, eyes fixed on the Deputy but legs making no attempt to carry her across the street. Without Rex she had nowhere to go in this new town, new *state*. Not now she knew he was the fiance she had travelled so far to meet.

She didn't - *couldn't* - marry a criminal, yet did she have a choice?

"Miss?"

She was jolted from her thoughts by a firm hand on her shoulder, firm enough to keep her rooted in place. "What?" she snapped - but when she tried to jerk free the man only tightened his grip.

"I will walk you to wherever you need to go. Perhaps then you will agree to let us spend some time together."

Did he *ever* stop? Once again she tried to wriggle from his grasp but he was so *strong,* hand gripping her with no effort at all. "Please, I need to leave," she replied - but she lacked the confidence she had tried to hard to convey.

"Now miss, don't you think your overreacting? I'm simply trying to help-"

"Mary? *Emmett?*"

She whipped her head to the side to see none other that Rex standing in the doorway, eyes wide and thick eyebrows raised. Oh no. She was supposed to be *gone* by the time he woke up - and now here he was, slowly stalking toward her with lips pursed in disapproval.

When his eyes met the man's - Emmett's - she realised it wasn't disapproval of *her.* "What are you doing here, Emmett?"

Emmett's grasp slackened as he stepped back; and then stumbled over the uneven, cobbled ground. "I should be asking *you.* I thought you were arrested yesterday." His eyes clouded in confusion - but then realisation hit. "That coach, with the Sheriff - *you* were inside."

Mary took the distraction to worm herself free and relief flooded her when he let her go without issue. She scrambled back, away from both men, pulse skipping. A million questions whirled in her mind but did she even want to know the answers? Despite this her lips parted and the question tumbled from her mouth without thought, "who *are* you two - and how do you know each other?"

"Why sweetheart, this idiot here is my brother," Emmett paused to glare at Rex, "do you wish to know why he was arrested? He stole from our father."

Oh. *Oh.* The revelation hit her like a physical slap and Mary let slip a *gasp* as a hand flew to her mouth.

"That isn't the whole truth," Rex snapped, voice dangerously low, "so I would appreciate if you didn't spread those lies."

Movement caught the corner of Mary's eyes - the Deputy had discarded his cigar. Even across the street she saw the suspicion on his young features, the tense way he held his shoulders. He was walking straight toward them.

Rex saw him too - and he froze for a moment, eyes narrowed into a deep scowl. "We need to leave," he muttered to Mary, "we've been seen."

"Now, don't think you can get away with-"

"We're leaving." Rex gave no opportunity for Emmett to finish or for Mary to protest. He took her by the arm - and she couldn't help but notice he was so much gentler than last night - and then they were on the move.

Rex knew the streets so intimately, and it was clear as they wound through streets and back roads, Rex leading expertly. It was as if he had memorised the town completely. Mary didn't protest - she was too breathless, her pulse hammering too fiercely in her throat.

Finally they stopped and Mary gulped in a breath, eager to steady her rapid heartbeat. When she turned to Rex he ignored her, head bowed as if embarrassed. She didn't ask. Instead she put a hand to his shoulder and said, "I don't think the Deputy followed us."

"Good."

She paused, wondering if she should say any more. After a moment she braced herself, taking in another heavy breath and asked, "What did you mean when you said it wasn't 'the whole truth'?"

With a scowl he shoved her gentle hand away and growled, "none of your business."

And that was all he said on the matter.

———————————————

The train station. It was where all this first began and now here she was, back again. Mary watched the crowd, eyes flickering from one face to the other. They all looked so happy, so content as they milled about, oblivious to everything but their own concerns.

"Come on. It's a quarter-past three; there's a train leaving in fifteen minutes."

Mary followed diligently but a frown slipped onto her slender features as she watched Rex squeeze between the crowd. He was rough and bad tempered - yet Mary found herself almost excited to climb onto that train with him. *Excited!* How absurd. She put it down to wanting adventure in her life, to needing to get away from her boring, bland old life. She didn't let herself consider another possibility.

"How can we afford this? I have nothing on me, not even a change of clothing - and you don't appear to have much either."

Rex scowled and Mary tensed, expecting him to dismiss her concerns as he always did - but then he sighed, deflating. Had he realised keeping secrets from her was only making it worse? "I still have the money I stole. Almost all of his money - enough to get out of here and start anew somewhere else."

There was another question on Mary's lips, an obvious one she couldn't voice. Her throat was dry, refusing to let the question escape.

It was still there in the back of her mind. *What kind of person steals from family?*

They moved in silence, working against the sea that was the crowd. Mary, average height at best, had to push past a group of men and one snapped a crude remark as she tried to inch past. Mary ignored him, focus entirely on Rex. It would have been easy to slip away unnoticed into the crowd, yet she didn't. She chalked it up to a combination of curiosity and the hope it would all turn out okay. Yes, that was absolutely it. It had nothing to do with Rex at all.

People had already began to board the train - women with their children, men carrying heavy suitcases, a group of women giggling as they climbed aboard. It was going to be full, perhaps without a single seat left to spare.

"Don't you think leaving town is only escalating the problem?" Mary asked, voice raised above the chatter of the train station. "Avoiding arrest, disappearing to another town - it's all a bit much, is it not?"

"I told you, I'm not going back to jail."

"No one wants to be in jail," she countered, "but then you shouldn't have stolen your father's money-"

He paused and whirled so quickly blonde hair flew into his eyes. "You know *nothing* of the situation. If I had not been caught you would never have known the difference, would have married me without a thought. Are you not in the wrong too, marrying a stranger for money?"

Mary tensed, her whole body seizing up as the urge to slap him took hold. She restrained, but it didn't stop the glare of narrowed eyes or the sharp intake of breath from her lips. "How *dare you*. If I remember correctly you approached me, *you* made the arrangements! Besides, it is hardly comparable to what you did."

By then people had started to move away with nervous glances or soft, mocking laughter. The station was quieter as people either parted or stopped to stare.

"Can we not do this? You're just embarrassing us both," Mary hissed. She attempted to stalk past him but he caught her wrist and tugged her back. She let out a yelp as she smacked against his chest - and then used slender hands to shove him away. "Why are you doing this?"

"Because you need to understand sometimes people make poor choices because they have to."

"How am I supposed to understand if you don't *explain?*" He was so secretive, avoiding her questions and then blowing up in her face when she pressed the matter. How she had ever thought him a kind and decent man she didn't know - she had disliked him from the moment they met, proving all of those letters were just fabricated nonsense. He wasn't even *close* to the husband he had promised to be-

The train whistled, shrill and pitched over the noise of the station. Mary's eyes snapped to the train, and then to the enormous clock on the wall. Half-past three - the train was leaving.

"We need to go *now.*"

Mary stood firm for a moment - and then she relaxed. She was giving in. What would her mother have said if she saw her now? Nothing good, that was for sure. She turned, dejected, ready to sprint for the train before it left - only to come face to face with someone so familiar it made her blood run cold.

Emmett; but not just Emmett - the Sheriff, the Deputy she had seen just that morning, and an older man with a dusting of greying hair.

Rex's hand landed on her shoulder; but it wasn't firm or demanding. This was something else, something *protective.* As if he were concerned.

"Rex," the older man spoke - and his voice mirrored Rex, deep and gruff but *angrier.* He smiled, but it was no more true than when

Emmett smiled at *her*. "I believe you have something that belongs to me."

The Sheriff stepped forward - and the crowd dispersed. Some slipped aside and some stumbled back as if they expected *they* were the ones in trouble. In only moments the sea parted, and it was just them.

"You can't run forever," Sheriff Woolford said with a weary sigh, "we've caught you now."

Mary shifted, allowing her gaze to drift from one person to the next. Emmett looked so *proud* and there was no doubt in her mind he had told the Sheriff. The Deputy too, must have known who they were and let the Sheriff know. Then there was the older man - Rex and Emmett's father - standing there stiff and silent, trying to look like a good, patient father. Something about his smile, the dullness in his eyes, told her something was wrong.

"Rex?" she questioned quietly.

He didn't answer - but he stared the Sheriff down with a glare that would make *anyone* shudder. "I won't go to jail, and I won't give back that money. It's rightfully *mine*."

Mary's brows flew to her hairline, eyes widening. *What* was he talking about? Was this another lie, another avoidance? With his stoic expression it was impossible to know.

"There's no need to make this more difficult for yourself," the Deputy supplied helpfully, "you can come with us without a fuss, or we can make you."

"No."

The train let out one last whining whistle - and then it was rolling out of the station with a deep rumble and a burst of smoke. There went their chance to leave, and Rex's chance to escape. Relief settled in her stomach but there was something else, a wariness for the situation at hand. Intuition told her perhaps there was more to this than she knew.

"Rex," his father supplied - and when he reached out a comforting hand Rex flinched back. *That* wasn't the reaction a man had to a father, even under these circumstances. "If you give me back the money and go with the Sheriff, there will be a place at home for you when you are released. Any parent would be right to disown you after this - but I will not hold this against you."

"Then it's a good thing you're no parent of mine-"

"*Rex!*" Emmett snapped, "Michael is just as much a father to you as your real one. How *dare you-*"

"That money is *mine,* Emmett! It was left to me by our father and *he,*" Rex jabbed a finger toward the man now known as Michael, "took it. If you were ever around instead of trying to pick up girls, you might have known. He's been nothing but cruel to me - and our mother - since they were married."

Silence. No one spoke - not Emmett, who's lips were firmly pursed; or Rex, who's body was trembling with rage; or even Michael, who's mouth stood agape but lost for words.

Then everything settled into place. The obscurity, the unwillingness to explain and the *fury* when Mary had mentioned who she thought was his father. Rex hadn't stolen a thing, only taken what he was denied.

"Men, I think we need to-"

"Wait," Mary silenced the Deputy before he could complete his thought. She stepped up to Rex with a soft smile and reached up to cup his face. "This really isn't your fault at all, is it? I am *so* sorry for the way I treated you; for demanding answers, for thinking you were a common criminal. I judged you to harshly."

His eyes narrowed and Mary expected him to reject her gentle touch - but then he leaned into her palm and smiled - the first smile she had seen and *goodness,* it was radiant.

"This is sweet and all," Sheriff Woolford interrupted with a cough, "but I would love to have this all explained to me."

Rex dipped down to press a kiss to Mary's cheek and her stomach fluttered, a smile spreading across her cheeks - but there was no time to dwell on it. They had to sort this out.

"Michael is my step-father," Rex replied coldly, "and when my father died he left most of his money to me. When my mother remarried Michael he took over the household and the finances - that meant everyone's money. Even mine."

"It was selfish of you to keep all that to yourself," Michael snapped, "you left, bought a house of your own and found a well paying job; you didn't need that money. *We* did."

"You spent a quarter of it on alcohol within the first year," Rex shot back, "so don't pretend it was for Mother."

The Sheriff sighed deeply, shoulders slouching. "I *did* wonder why you were suddenly frequenting the saloon so often," he admitted. Then, "I think there's been a misunderstanding. Rex, if you had only mentioned this when we first arrested you-"

"It's *embarrassing,* all right?" he growled, "to admit, even as a fully grown man, I had allowed someone to control me for so long. Then the crash happened, I panicked - and I also realised it was the excuse I needed to leave and start up somewhere new."

Mary kept quiet - but the uneasiness inside of her refused to leave. She shifted, eyes drifting to Rex. She dropped her gaze as soon as he looked over.

The station had begun to fill up again and it was soon confirmed why - another train pulled up, rumbling along slowly. Mary's heart skipped as she realised their chance to leave wasn't torn from them forever; only if they failed to leave with this train. Excitement filled her, and relief - relief that Rex wasn't who she thought, that he was innocent and she could *still* have a life with him. Perhaps. Right now, she just wanted them to be left alone.

Her wish might just be granted. Sheriff Woolford sighed once more, like the energy had been drained from him. When he spoke, it was directed to Emmett. "Is this all true?"

As if he was going to take their side. He was rude and arrogant, selfish-

"It is," he admitted quietly, "Michael has controlled Rex and our mother since the beginning; I only avoided it by moving out before he married Mother." He ducked his head, embarrassed and ashamed. "Everything is true."

"Well," the Deputy clapped his hands, ignoring how Michael glared at him, "then Rex is innocent, and we can go home happy."

"First of all, we have to take you to the Sheriff's office," Sheriff Woolford addressed Michael - and then he was securing his grasp around Michael's hands and towing him away. "I'm sorry about all of this you two, truly. If you leave now you might still get that train."

Mary watched them leave - the Sheriff and Michael first, and then the Deputy. Emmett lingered, gaze downcast, and eventually he left without a word.

The buzz of the station swam back into focus and then it was all she could hear, the white noise of hundreds of voices all mingled together.

When Rex spoke, though, it rose above all else. "Do you want to go? After all this, I won't stop you from leaving."

Her reply was instant as warmth bloomed in her chest. She had been so wrong about him, but now she knew the *truth;* and she knew she wanted to marry him. "I'll go wherever you do."

"One thing first." He smiled but hesitated - lingering with a hand out as if to cup her cheek. Mary had to urge him on but then he bent down, lips brushing gently across hers. Then he scooped her by the waist and pulled her close. His lips moved against hers and she let out a breathless little laugh against the kiss.

And that kiss, really, signified everything. Their journey had been ridiculous and terrifying but here they were kissing in an overcrowded train station, about to leave for somewhere new and never look back.

Despite it all, Mary didn't want anything else.

BLOSSOMING AMISH

Chapter One

Abigail Schroder awoke to the sound of birds chirping outside of her bedroom window.

Abigail took a deep breath and let out a sad sigh. Pulling herself up in bed, she propped her back against her pillow and watched as the birds worked side-by-side to craft a home for their future family.

While she generally loved to tiptoe over to the glass and watch as the pair of happy bluebirds worked together building a nest, this morning was different. Today their merry song only brought to mind her own misery.

The birds had always reminded her of what her future life would be like. She had dreamed of a life where she and her husband would work hand-in-hand to raise up a family in their Amish community.

Now, all of Abigail's dreams had been shattered.

"Jacob," she whispered the name gently, wishing that the past two months had been

nothing more than a dream.

Jacob had been her beau since the couple had met at a young people's gathering. For the past five years they had dated.

Abigail had planned to spend her entire life by Jacob's side. She had wanted to marry him, raise children with him, and then grow old along with him.

But now it was all gone.

She had been so hopeful the night Jacob had asked to see her alone. There had been something different about him. Rather than taking her to an Amish gathering or somewhere on a date, he told her that he just wanted to talk.

After five years together, Abigail could only imagine that he was going to ask for her to marry him. She had spent the entire day with a smile on her face as she did the regular chores of hanging laundry out to dry, scrubbing the floors, and helping her two younger sisters sew new dresses.

Abigail wasn't the only one who hoped for the best. Her fourteen-year-old sister Sally had begged her to tell her what happened first, and she had noticed a spark of excitement in her parents' eyes when Jacob arrived on his buggy.

She and Jacob had laughed together as they drove out to their favorite spot on the back of his *daed's* farm. Sitting together, they watched the sun go down while butterflies danced around them.

"Abigail," Jacob had whispered as she leaned her head against his shoulder and closed her eyes, "I have something I need to tell you."

It had been different than Abigail had expected. The words sounded wrong in her ears and, rather than seeming happy, Jacob's voice sounded strained.

She had looked up at him and watched as the man she had loved for so long forced a sad smile.

"I'm leaving, Abigail." He announced the words she had never expected to hear.

"Leaving?" She had repeated, "What do you mean?"

"I'm leaving the Amish," Jacob had announced with a shrug. When he looked down at her surprise he laughed, "Come on, girl. We've been together for five years. You knew it was going to happen eventually! I don't belong here! I'm not like anyone in the community and I don't want to be."

"Jacob," Abigail had tried to change his mind, "Our future..."

"Exactly," he had interrupted, "I want a future outside of a dirty chicken farm. I want to see the world. I want to be able to drive a car and wear normal clothes. I want to be able to talk on a phone and watch television without fear of getting in trouble. I want to be free, Abigail. I want to wipe the dirt of this place and these people off my hands. I want to try being whoever Jacob wants to be!"

"What about us?" Abigail's voice had sounded like no more than a whisper.

Jacob looked down and shook his head, "Abigail...there is no more us."

That had been it. Abigail had tried to convince him to stay with the Amish community, but all she could do was cry as he drove her home.

Even now, two months later, Abigail could hardly stop the tears from rolling down her cheeks as she watched the pair of birds working together outside of her window.

"Abigail," she heard her mother's familiar voice along with a soft rap against her bedroom door, "It's time to be up. Church will begin soon. I need your help with breakfast."

"Coming, Mom," Abigail managed to call out. She scooted down in bed and closed her eyes, trying to erase all her thoughts.

Church. If there was one place that she didn't want to go, it was church. Every two weeks the Amish community gathered in a different home to perform the service that started in the morning and ended with a group meal. Growing up, Abigail had loved the Sunday ritual, but now it was one of her least favorite parts of the week.

With the loss of Jacob, it felt as if Abigail had also lost all her faith in God. She had spend the last five years of her life so sure of her future, and now it felt that it had all been ripped away from her. And now, at twenty-three-years-old, Abigail found that she was one of the oldest singles in her Amish community. It appeared that her dream to be a wife and a mother was gone for good.

It seemed God no longer had a plan or a use for Abigail Schroder.

Chapter Two

While Abigail would rather have stayed home from church, she realized that this was not an option. Although her parents had been very understanding of her heartbreak, they were unyielding where church was concerned.

"God still has a plan for you, Abigail," her *mamm* would assure her any time that Abigail would mention her lack of spiritual fervor.

So, that Sunday morning, Abigail found herself squeezed onto one of the hard wooden benches in John Yoder's house. She glanced at her sisters, Sally and Emma, who sat on either side of her. They seemed completely engrossed in the message that the preacher was providing.

"I know the plans I have for you," The preacher was reading from the Bible, "Plans to prosper you and not to harm you, plans to give you a future and a hope."

Abigail shut her eyes and tried to will herself not to cry.

God no longer had a plan for her. She knew that. All her dreams had been erased when Jacob left. Life seemed completely pointless now and the future only dark and empty.

When the preacher had finished his message, the family joined the rest of the church for a large meal out in the barn. The Yoders had provided enough food for the entire congregation with baked chicken, homemade noodles, gravy, and potatoes. While she knew the food was delicious, Abigail could hardly force herself to eat.

As she shifted her food across her plate with her fork, she thought of services past. Services when Jacob had been by her side, amusing her with his funny stories from work and making her laugh at his constant antics. How she missed him!

"Abigail," she was brought out of her thoughts when her sister Emma gave her a gentle nudge with her elbow, "Abigail, who is that man?"

Abigail looked up from her plate of food and in the direction that Emma was pointing. Sitting several tables over was a young Amish man that she didn't recognize. He was tall and thin with a shock of dark hair. Looking up, his brown eyes met Abigail's before she could look back down at her plate.

"Who is he?" Emma asked again.

Abigail shrugged her shoulders, "I have no idea."

Recently, many new couples had been moving into their community with their families.

Families...the word alone made Abigail want to cry.

She would never have a family of her own.

Looking back, she should have realized that things with Jacob had never been good. In their five years together, he had never once mentioned marriage, even while all their other friends had been tying the knot. Jacob had only ever been interested in having fun. He liked to have his own way and always got what he wanted.

The realization that Abigail had simply been someone for him to use for his enjoyment was almost more than she could stand. While she had been planning her future with him, to Jacob she was simply a stepping stone to his life apart from her.

"Pete, Lovina," She heard a voice speaking to her parents, "I have someone I want you to meet."

Abigail looked up in time to see their bishop introducing her parents to the stranger Emma had pointed out.

"This is Noah Abrams," the bishop was explaining, "He's new to the community."

Noah nodded his head and stretched out his hand to take her father's, "Mr. Schroder, it's good to meet you and your family."

Abigail's father smiled and said, "It's good to have you in the community, Noah! I'd like you to meet my wife, Lovina, and our daughters, Sally, Emma, and Abigail."

Noah nodded his head to each of the girls. It seemed to Abigail that his gaze paused on her. Staring into his dark chocolate eyes was almost more than she could bear and she had to look down at her lap.

"Oh, Abigail," Sally breathed softly as the bishop led him on to speak to someone else, "Where do you suppose his wife is? Do you think he's married? It's hard to imagine that anyone that *wunderbar gut* looking would be single!"

Abigail gave her sister a solemn glance and then continued to play with her food.

It was true, the stranger was handsome. His body was so tall and fit, his dark hair so wavy, and his eyes so incredibly deep. When he had looked at her, Abigail almost felt as if Noah Abrams could look into her very soul.

"*Ach*, Abigail," she scolded herself silently, "You better stop."

Surely looking at men was not a good idea for Abigail. When Jacob had left so had all hopes of her future; it was time she accepted that truth completely. Besides, Noah Abrams was probably married.

Chapter Three

Monday morning was the start of a new week and the day that Abigail went to go help out Mandy Eicher. Mandy was the Amish community's seamstress. Each week she took on sewing and, with her youngest daughter recently married, the workload was more than Mandy could handle on her own.

Despite the beautiful spring weather, the five-minute walk to the Eicher house left Abigail feeling morose. She wondered if this was to be the rest of her life. She wondered if each day she would do the same thing until she was an old maid.

Wiping a tear from her eye, Abigail softly whispered, "Why, Lord? What kind of life am I going to lead? If this is all you have planned for me and I am never to have the dearest wishes of my heart, why did you give me life at all?"

Abigail didn't knock on Mandy's door; instead, she simply turned the knob and stepped into the backroom where Mandy worked on the sewing.

Surprisingly enough, Mandy was not at her old fashioned sewing machine yet and the pile of laundry was still lying untouched on the table.

"Hmmm," Abigail whispered to herself, "This isn't like the Mandy that I know."

"Mandy," she called out as she started to sort through a pile of dresses, "Mandy, are ya home?"

Suddenly, the form of a little girl came scampering into the sewing room, filling the area with her giggles.

"Hi!" She greeted Abigail, a huge smile stretched across her pretty round face, "What's your name?"

Abigail raised her eyebrows in surprise. While she knew that Mandy had several grandchildren, she had never met this child before.

"I'm Abigail." Despite Abigail's sad mood, something about the little girl instantly warmed her heart.

The child pushed back a blonde curl that had escaped from her prayer cap and smiled, "Well, it's good to meet you, Abigail! My name is Katie and I'm five years old."

She seemed like such a little lady that Abigail couldn't help but smile back. She wanted to pick Katie up and give her a hug.

"You're nice," Katie announced.

"Where are your parents?" Abigail asked as she foraged through her pocket and pulled out a piece of candy to offer the child.

"Ooohhh, candy!" Katie squealed as she took the piece of peppermint, "*Danki*, Abigail! My *daed* had to go work on our new house today, so I have to stay here with Aunt Mandy."

"What about your mama?"

Katie shrugged sadly, her face suddenly clouding over, "I never had one...but I want one awful badly! Daddy says that we just have to wait on God to bring us a new one, but He sure is taking a long time. I'm starting to wonder if God ever wants me to get a new *Mamm*!"

"Oh, there you are!" Mandy let out a sigh of relief as she stepped into the room, "Katie, I have been looking all over the house for you! Where have you been?"

The little girl shrugged her shoulders, "Right here, Aunt Mandy!"

Mandy shook her head and took a deep breath, "*Gut* morning, Abigail. I am so sorry to keep you waiting. It's been a long time since I've had a little child around the house." Putting her hand on Katie's head, Mandy went on to say, "She's my great-niece. Katie and her dad just moved to the community and he's working to build a house. I've agreed to let them stay here and watch her during the day until his house gets finished..." Mandy took a deep breath and let it out, "I'm really not sure what he will do with her after that."

Abigail had always respected Mandy but hearing her talk of Katie as if she was nothing more than a burden broke her heart.

Katie got down on the floor to chase after a glass marble as Mandy went on to announce, "His wife died when Katie was born. If he had any sense, he would have remarried then. As things are now, he has no one to watch Katie and no hopes of things ever getting better!"

Abigail watched the little girl and shook her head sadly. It was strange to think that she wasn't the only one whose heart had been broken by loss. She knew what it was like to love someone and then lose them.

"Do you want me to get started on sewing one of these dresses?" Abigail asked softly as she motioned toward the pile of clothes.

Mandy shook her head, "Actually, I have a better use for you today, Abigail. I'll do most of the sewing if you'll just keep up with Katie. Would you mind?"

Would she mind? Abigail could think of no better job in the world!

Chapter Four

Often, Abigail found working at Mandy's to be a bit of a drag. The piles of clothing seemed never-ending and the hours would pass so slowly. Today, however, things were different.

Keeping up with Katie was the most enjoyable job that Abigail had ever done. She played hide-n-go-seek with the little girl, they baked cookies together, and they went out to the barn to look at the calves.

As the hours of the afternoon started to fade away, Abigail took Katie inside and helped her sew a little pincushion from some leftover scraps of material.

"You are a wonder with that child," Mandy announced with a smile as she watch Katie sitting quietly on the floor playing with the pincushion she had just made, "I thought I would pull my hair out before you came today!"

"She's a treasure," Abigail replied.

She was going to say more, but suddenly the voice of men interrupted her thoughts. Mandy's husband had returned home and with him was someone else.

"Aunt Mandy, where are you?"

"Back here!"

"It's Daddy!" Katie announced as she jumped up from her place on the floor, "Daddy, Daddy, come here!"

The figure of a tall man stepped into the sewing room and Katie went running to his side, "Daddy, Daddy, pick me up! I've got something to show you!"

Noah Abrams.

Abigail knew it was him as soon as she heard his voice. Although she had only seen him for a few minutes at church, it seemed she had memorized him instantly.

"Ah, a pincushion," he was exclaiming as he looked over Katie's project, "You'll have to be careful when playing with pins!"

"That's what Abigail already told me," Katie laughed as her father tickled her chin, "She's the nice lady who helped me!"

Noah finally looked up and let his eyes meet Abigail's. With a smile of recognition, he nodded his head, "Abigail Schroder, right?"

Abigail found herself tempted to look down at the floor in sudden awkwardness, "That's right."

"Abigail saved me today, Noah," Mandy was quick to announce as she cut a piece of thread on a pair of pants and put them aside, "I was able to get so much more work done while she kept Katie entertained."

"Abigail is so much fun!" Katie said with a smile before turning to Abigail, "Abigail are you going to come back to play with me tomorrow?"

"No, I'm afraid not." Abigail almost hated to tell the little girl, "I only come help your Aunt Mandy on Mondays and Fridays."

Katie's little smile quickly turned into a frown, "But I want you to come back!"

"Katie," Noah scolded gently, "Don't be rude. Miss Abigail may have other things she needs to do. You'll see her soon. Now tell her good night and go get washed up for supper."

Katie tried to smile, but her chin quivered as she got out of her father's arms and went over to give Abigail a hug.

"Bye, Abigail," the little girl whispered, "I hope you'll come back to see me again."

Mandy led Katie out of the room to go get ready for supper, leaving Noah and Abigail alone.

They stood alone in awkward silence until Abigail finally started to gather her things.

"Well," Abigail took a deep breath, "Until Friday, I suppose."

"I didn't see a buggy when I pulled up." Noah said before Abigail could reach the door, "Do you have a driver coming?"

Abigail shook her head, "I walk home."

"Don't do that. My buggy is still hitched up. I can give you a ride back while I wait on Aunt Mandy to get supper."

Abigail wanted to protest but Noah stopped her.

"No 'buts'," he announced with a smile, "I should do something to repay you for your kindness to my little girl."

With a nod, Abigail found herself agreeing and allowed Noah Abrams to lead her out to his buggy.

Chapter Five

Abigail had not been alone with a man since Jacob left. Even though her house was just down the road, she wondered if she could bear the trip.

"I'm glad we could get a chance to talk," Noah announced as he guided his horse down the gravel drive that led to the road, "Truth be told, I'm at my wits end now that I'm here at my aunt's house. Until I get my own home finished, I have to leave Katie there and Aunt Mandy simply doesn't have the energy needed to take care of a little girl."

Abigail nodded sympathetically, "What do you plan to do?"

"Oh, things will be fine once I get my house finished and my farm up and running. I'm used to taking care of Katie. I just can't build a house with her by my side. A worksite isn't a safe place for a five-year-old."

Although Katie was a sweet child, Abigail tried to imagine how hard it would be for this poor man to try to care for her while running a farm.

"I honestly don't see how you do it all alone," Abigail announced before she could think better of her words, "It must be difficult with no wife."

Suddenly, Abigail felt her face growing warm. She wondered if her embarrassment was showing. Surely her ears must be as red as the beets that grew in her mom's garden.

"It is very rough," Noah replied with a sigh, "Even after all these years, it isn't always easy. Sometimes I doubt my ability to raise a little girl on my own but it seems to be the job that God has given me."

Abigail braved a glance at the man beside her. He looked so solemn, so completely resigned to his future. Abigail could tell that Noah Abrams had faced many difficulties in his life.

"Miss Schroder," Noah began, his voice sounding almost nervous, "I know you're too busy to even consider it, but, until I get my house finished, I need a babysitter for Katie. My aunt just can't seem to do it anymore. Would you be willing to take on the job?"

Would she?! Abigail had to fight to keep from clapping her hands in excitement. The idea of going a whole week without seeing Katie had made life seem so hollow; his job offer truly seemed like an answer to her prayers.

"Yes," She replied without any hesitation, "I can't think of anything I would love any more!"

Noah looked to Abigail and smiled. In that instant, it seemed that a weight had been lifted off his shoulders. Suddenly, he seemed carefree and happy, and whistled the rest of the way to the Schroder house.

Noah started picking Abigail up in his buggy every morning and taking her to his aunt's house where she would spend the day watching little Katie. Each day that passed, the small child became even more dear to Abigail and, surprisingly enough, so did Noah.

Abigail certainly wasn't allowing herself to entertain ideas about the handsome young widower, but she couldn't deny that a tiny shoot of hope was beginning to grow in her heart. Just like the tiny beans that had sprouted in the garden, Abigail was beginning to feel like her heart was thawing and that perhaps there was room for someone other than Jacob.

Chapter Six

Abigail had been watching little Katie daily for six weeks when Noah arrived at her house one bright Tuesday morning with a certain mischievous grin on his face. Unlike most mornings, he had small daughter at his side and a wicker basket loaded into the back of the wagon.

"*Gut* morning, Abigail!" Noah exclaimed as he reached out to help her up onto the seat, "Are you ready for a big adventure?"

Katie was grinning from ear-to-ear, leaving Abigail to wonder exactly what was up Noah Abram's sleeve.

"I don't know," Abigail replied with a laugh as she settled down on the other side of Katie, "I'm never very adventurous. What do you have planned?"

"You'll see," Noah promised with a wink.

To Abigail's surprise, Noah drove his buggy past Mandy's house and on down the road.

"Where are we going?" Katie asked, her confusion making it obvious that she was just as uncertain about the day as Abigail.

"Wait and see," Noah said as he wrapped an arm around his little child's shoulder.

Together, the three of them traveled down a small country road and turned onto a gravel driveway lined with blossoming apple trees.

"It's so beautiful!" Katie squealed as she reached out to try to touch one of the pink blossoms, "Where are we going, Daddy? This can't be the regular world, can it, Abigail?"

It certainly didn't feel like the regular world, even to Abigail. It felt like they were entering a magical land where dreams came true. Abigail took a deep breath, drawing in the scent of the wildflowers growing in the surrounding meadows. This felt like a place where she could finally release all the pain from her past and leave her worries behind.

"Look up there," Noah pointed ahead of them.

There at the end of the driveway, was a huge two-story white farmhouse.

"Oh, Daddy," Katie breathed softly, "Who owns this house?"

"We do, sweetheart!"

The house was beautiful, but it wasn't what held Abigail's attention. Instead, she found herself staring at Noah as he chatted with his daughter about their new home. It was the first time Abigail had seen him so happy. His dark brown eyes were glimmering and he was smiling like a little boy. Something about him was captivating.

Noah stopped the buggy beside the house and hopped down from his seat.

"This is it," He kept repeating as he led Katie and Abigail up onto the porch, "Sure, it's not quite finished yet. It will probably be another week before we can move in, but this is it! We have a home!"

"We have a home!" Katie repeated as she jumped up and down, clapping her hands together, "Did you hear that Abigail, we have a home!"

Abigail didn't even find herself shying away or correcting the little girl's mistake; the moment was simply too precious and Abigail discovered that she truly wished that this was her home as well.

They spend the day touring the large house and looking over the property. Noah had purchased two-hundred acres and explained his plans to build various barns to hold different animals along with his hopes to plant different kinds of grain.

Each moment that passed, Abigail found herself falling a little more in love with the man before her.

Certainly, Noah was not Jacob, but he was so much more. Selfless, caring, and gentle, Abigail wished that she had been able to meet Noah first.

Chapter Seven

Noah finished the afternoon off with a picnic by the side of the creek that trickled through his property. He had packed a delicious lunch of fried chicken, mashed potatoes, and strawberries.

"Daddy," Katie jumped up as soon as she had finished her last bite, "Can I go play in the water?"

Noah nodded, "Of course!"

Katie giggled with excitement as she hurried down to the bubbling water.

"Is she safe by herself?" Abigail asked, wondering if she should go along.

Noah nodded, "We can see her from here and the creek is only an inch deep."

Of course, Noah knew everything about the safety of the property. Abigail let out a sigh of relief as she leaned back on her elbows. She just wanted to sit peacefully and soak in the day. She wished that this afternoon never had to end.

"This is the prettiest place I've ever seen," Abigail commented.

Noah smiled, "I've always dreamed of living on a farm like this. Back in Ohio, I had a nice place, but it was just functional. I want Katie to grow up on a farm like this. It was what Lizzy wanted too..." Suddenly, his voice trailed off and his happy smile was totally replaced by something much more sober.

"Was Lizzy your wife?" Abigail ventured to ask, wondering if she should even tackle a subject that obviously brought him so much pain.

Noah nodded his head and started absentmindedly pulling pieces of grass out of the ground, "Lizzy and I got together when we were sixteen years old, and got married before we turned twenty. She was a good girl, Abigail. She had my whole heart in a way I never thought anyone else ever could..."

"What happened?"

Noah's gaze turned to the creek where his little girl was playing, "Katie happened. We wanted a baby so much, but it seems that Lizzy wasn't strong enough to handle a pregnancy. There were so many complications. When Katie was born, there was trouble and she had to go stay in the hospital. She only lived for one night." Noah shook his head, "I promised her so many things, Abigail. Promises that, sometimes, I'm not sure that I can keep. Sometimes I'm so scared that I'm going to fail her."

Noah reached up and brushed a tear away from his cheek. Watching his pain made Abigail's heart ache.

"Noah," she said in little more than a whisper, "I think you're doing everything right."

Noah turned to look at her. His eyes were red from fighting back his tears.

"*Ach*, Abigail," he muttered, "You know exactly how to help me."

In an unexpected turn of events, he reached out and gently cradled Abigail's face in his large hand.

"Daddy!" Katie's voice interrupted them, and Noah quickly withdrew.

"Daddy, Abigail, look!" Katie squealed as she came running toward their picnic spot, "I caught a fish!"

She held out her fist and revealed a tiny minnow that she had caught in the creek, "Can we cook him for supper?"

Noah and Abigail looked at each other and burst into laughter. Their special moment was over, but Abigail felt as if something between them had certainly changed forever.

Chapter Eight

Before taking her home, Noah stopped by Mandy's house.

"I'm going to take Katie in so she can go on and get ready for bed," he explained as he helped the little girl down from the buggy.

"I'll go in and say hello to your aunt," Abigail said as she took his hand in hers to get down from her seat.

Noah took Katie back into her bedroom to get changed for bed and Abigail started toward the sewing room.

As she neared the sewing room door, she could hear Mandy's voice, "Noah's almost done with his house," she was saying, "I'll be so glad once he moves out!"

Abigail lifted her hand to knock against the door, but stopped when she heard another voice speak up, "Have you seen the way that Abigail throws herself at your nephew?"

"*Ach,* yes," Abigail could see Mandy shaking her head sadly through a crack in the door, "I'm afraid that the poor girl is simply in for even more heartbreak. After being jilted by Jacob back in the spring, she must be so desperate!"

"So you don't think Noah has any interest in her?"

Mandy let out a disgusted laugh, "Most certainly not! He's used her as a babysitter, but he's had women help him out before. My sister said one girl in Ohio was almost certain that he would propose...as soon as he heard the rumors, he let her go."

Rachel Miller was clucking her tongue in condescending sadness.

"I wish he would, but Noah will never marry. He made a promise to his wife and that's final. I just wish he'd stop leading these poor girls to believe there is hope!" Mandy continued on, but Abigail couldn't bear to listen anymore. Instead, she turned and silently hurried out the side door, unwilling to wait for Noah to take her home.

Abigail couldn't stop the flood of tears that kept running down her cheeks. She wondered if she could even make it back to her house before she completely fell apart.

She could hear footsteps behind her, their sound only making it worse as she realized that she was being followed.

"Abigail," Noah called out as he ran up behind her, "Abigail, what's wrong?"

"Nothing!" Abigail exclaimed bitterly as she wrapped her arms across her chest, "I feel sick. I've got to get home."

With longer legs, Noah quickly overtook her.

"Abigail," he exclaimed as stood in front of her to block her way, "Can't I at least take you home? You've been crying! Why are you so upset? What has happened?"

"Nothing!" Abigail insisted as she stomped her foot against the ground, "Just let me go!"

When Noah saw that there was nothing he could do to stop her, he stepped out of the way and let Abigail pass.

How could I have been so foolish? Abigail asked herself as she marched down the road toward her house, *I should have never trusted another man! I should have never trusted God to have a plan for me!*

The next morning, Abigail stayed home from work. When Noah came to pick her up, she had her sister Sally go with him instead.

Chapter Nine

Each minute of the day had been agony. She had missed Katie, and she had missed Noah. How she had come to look forward to their time together! Abigail already found herself missing Noah much more than she had ever missed Jacob.

Abigail was out in the chicken house gathering eggs and trying not to cry when she heard a buggy pull into their yard.

Stepping out to check on who might be visiting, she was surprised to see Noah's buggy. On the seat beside him were Sally and Katie.

"Why are they home so early?" Abigail wondered to herself. She had planned to hide away inside the house when they returned, making it impossible to be faced with seeing him. Now she had no way to escape.

Noah scanned the yard as he helped both her sister and Katie down from the buggy.

"Where is Abigail?" She could hear the little girl ask.

"I don't know," Sally replied, "But you can come inside and we'll look for her. I'll also give you a piece of chocolate cake!"

Noah's eyes were scanning the property. When he turned to look her way, Abigail grabbed for the chicken house door, ready to hide wherever she could; however, she wasn't fast enough. In an instant, Noah's eyes were locked on her.

"Abigail, wait!" He exclaimed, making large strides in her direction, "We have to talk!"

"There's nothing to talk about."

Noah was now by her side.

"Abigail," Noah took a deep breath and caught her hand in his, "What's wrong? I thought that you were having a good time taking care of little Katie. Why would you want to quit now?"

"You don't understand, do you?" Abigail shook her head sadly, "I can't do it anymore, Noah! I just can't!"

"Why? If it's because of what happened on the picnic, I am truly sorry. I acted out of hast and I shouldn't have. I should never have touched you..."

Abigail shook her head. She couldn't let Noah think that she was rejecting him.

"No, no, no!" She exclaimed, closing her eyes and trying to keep the tears from pouring like rain, "It's not that at all. Oh, Noah, you don't understand. I overheard your aunt talking. She said that you will never get married again, that your wife made you promise that you wouldn't! I can't stand to lose you, Noah, I just can't! I love you far too much for that. If we can't ever be together, than I can't be around you at all!"

Noah let out something that sounded almost like a sigh of relief, "Abigail, dear Abigail," he reached up and gently brushed away her tears with the tip of his finger, "I thought that you hated me. You poor, dear girl! My aunt knows some things, but she doesn't know everything. When Lizzy died, she did make me promise things. She made me promise that I would take care of Katie, that I would love her, that I would do what was best for her, that I would give her a good home...and then she made me promise that I would not marry again until I found someone who I truly love, someone who will take good care of our little girl and who will take good care of me. Abigail, I have avoided women for that very reason. I have never felt like God had put the right one in my path. I never felt like any woman I met would ever be able to fill the void that Lizzy left in my heart."

His words...they almost gave her hope. Abigail took a deep breath and shook her head, "Noah, I know you can never feel that way about me."

Noah put his hands on her shoulders and stared into her eyes, "Abigail, you don't know how special you've become to me."

Suddenly, the words broke something deep inside of Abigail. It felt like the wall she had built around her heart was suddenly shattered into a million pieces as she realized that she truly did have hope.

"It can be hard to explain what is in my heart," Noah whispered as he leaned his forehead against hers, "But you need to know that what is in my heart is you, Abigail Schroder."

"Oh Noah," she whispered the words softly against his lips, "You are my whole heart as well."

Suddenly, their lips met in love's first kiss. As Noah pulled her closer against his strong body, Abigail could feel her broken heart begin to heal. Just when she thought that God had given up on her future, He had continued to work out His plans in her life. When Abigail had been ready to give up on ever having her own family, God had brought this wonderful *gut* man to her side.

Once their kiss was over, Abigail found herself leaning her head against this dear man's shoulder.

"Noah," she whispered gently, "Oh, Noah, I do love you so."

Suddenly, the sound of childish laughter brought them back to reality as Katie emerged from the large farmhouse and started bouncing across the yard.

"Daddy," Katie squealed as she ran to him and wrapped her arms around his legs, "Does this mean I'm going to get a new *Mamm*?"

Noah looked at Abigail and winked.

"It just might," he told her as he scooped the little girl up into his arms, "We will just have to ask her." Turning to look at Abigail, Noah asked, "Miss Schroder, would you do us the honor of being Katie's new *Mamm*? And my new wife?"

Abigail could hardly speak over the pounding of her joyful heart, "Nothing would make me any happier!"

She reached out and wrapped her arms around both Noah and Katie, pulling her new family close against her.

God truly had a plan after all.

GREY CLOUDS, NO RAIN

Chapter 1

Rain just kept falling, never ending without any intention to stop, large puddles had gathered on the muddy grounds around the big barn, and water gushed down the eroded embankment running alongside the road, causing the road to be completely flooded. But no amount of rain would prevent Amity, Betty and Rachel to do what they came here to do. Having been friends since childhood, the three women were inseparable. Neither of them were married or promised to anyone yet, and although they are well beyond the age most girls in their community starts to settle down to start a family, it never really bothered them.

Amity was strong willed and mouthy young woman, who voiced her opinion whenever she felt it mattered. Of course her father, Bishop Gunther didn't quite approve of her behaviour at times, but he did support her willingness to stand up for herself. Bishop Gunther on the other hand wasn't like most others in their faith; he was more lenient and accepting than most, always promoting change within reason. He insisted that households started using gas stoves instead of coal stoves. He had even arranged to buy a truck to help the community to cart goods to the local market in town. According to him, modern change to a bare minimum does not give the devil a foothold, it just shows the devil that they are capable of change without modern ways ruling their lives and changing who they are or distracting them from things that matter most.

Betty, much like Amity also had a strong personality, one she definitely got from her mother, but she also had a mischievous streak. When the elders instructed the children not to play in the rain, she was always the first to splash in muddy puddles. When they had their social events, she was the one who would pull pranks, like stuff a mouse in someone's pocket or stick a dish to a table cloth with workman's glue, causing a huge disaster when someone tries to pick it up. All innocent pranks at most, but that was how everyone knew her and more often than not, when she was younger her father would ground her for punishment, but she always found a way out of it.

And then there was Rachel, shy quiet Rachel. More like the runt of the litter, she was one of few words and always just tagged along because Amity and Betty insisted. Rachel only had a father; her mother died giving birth to her. Her father eventually married Elsa, a widow with two sons, who she never got on with. They were two brats and she ended up spending more time with her friends than her own family and over the years, the trio had become the best of friends

Betty giggled and Amity squirmed on the bale of hay, "I bet you David looks like that when he takes his shirt off," she said pointing to the male model in the fashion magazine.

Amity giggled, "It's scandalous! If your dad knew you had these, he'll shun us all," she said in jest.

Rachel, curious as ever, was sitting on the left, also peeking at the magazine, one of the few they kept hidden in the barn under one of the wooden floor slats. They always snuck to the barn to page through the magazines and weigh every other man in their town up against the likes of models that posed so shamelessly with nothing but pair of underpants on.

"*Jah!* Well he doesn't know now does he?" Betty said and paged through a few more pages.

Rachel would never admit it out rightly but she also felt a slight tingle of excitement when she looked at these magazines, they were not overly crude, but they showed more flesh than she had ever seen in her life. Maybe it was because of this, that they were all still single, she thought. Comparing the local boys to those men were like comparing apples with onions.

A sudden noise quickly alerted them and Betty shoved the magazine behind the bale of hay they were seated on. Both Amity and Betty grabbed their egg baskets, while Rachel stood around looking as guilty as ever.

"Betty, are you girls here?"

It was Betty's father who called, and Rachel's stomach lurched, if the Bishop had any idea what they were up to they will be in so much trouble.

"We're here *daed*!" Betty called and dusted the hay off of her dress, "We were caught in the rain, and was waiting for it to pass," she said as her Bishop Gunther appeared.

"I thought so, well I have come to get you girls home, the storm is a long way from being over," he said and handed each of them a rain coat, "Better we hurry, or the storm will catch up with us," he urged them as he let each one of the girls walk towards the barn door ahead of him.

The sky was dark and it wasn't just a summer shower, it was a downpour that looked more like a waterfall from heaven. Heavy drops struck the ground tunnelling into the earth. Up ahead stood the buggy, which didn't offer much or any shelter and Rachel wasn't so sure if they would make it to their respective homes in one piece. Betty was the first to step into the rain, followed by Amity. Bishop Gunther looked at her and nodded, and then in a huddled group the four of them ran towards the buggy, careful not to slip and fall.

Thankful that there was still some daylight to guide the way, the three girls clung to each other as Betty's father steered the buggy towards the house. Hardly able to see a few feet ahead of them and on a treacherous road that has been washed away in most places, Bishop Gunther was still able to make them feel at ease. He didn't even look worried, but then again, that was probably how a man of God should be, like Paul walking on water.

The buggy wheels rattled as they rode over rocks and muddy trenches formed by the mass of water running diagonally across the small road. And a trip that normally took less than fifteen minutes to travel, now seemed like an eternity. They were slowly making their way ahead through the stormy downpour, unbeknownst to Bishop Gunther, the road up ahead had turned into complete sludge and the moment the buggy reached it, the wheels simply slid into a deep trench on the side of the road, pulling the buggy, with the horse off and on to the side of the road. The girls screamed in panic as the buggy slowly leaned over to its side, threatening to topple over. Rachel was the first to clobber out and then helped the other two on to the road. Betty got out safely, but as Amity stumbled out of the buggy, she stepped in a hole and twisted her ankle.

"Ow!!" she cried out as she fell to the ground grabbing for her ankle.

"Amity!" Betty cried and ducked down to help her friend, "Where does it hurt?"

Bishop Gunther also hunched down and looked at her ankle, "It's quite swollen, I think you may have sprained it, can you try and step on it?"

Betty and her father helped Amity to her feet, but the moment she put weight on her injury, she cried out in agony.

"We will have to get you home, just lean on me and Betty" the Bishop said. He studied the state of the buggy, "The buggy will have to stay here until morning."

"But papa, we can hardly see in front of us," Betty lamented as she supported her friend.

"The Lord will light our way," Rachel said confidently and gave Betty a gentle reassuring squeeze.

With Amity supported by Bishop Gunther and Betty, and Rachel next to them carrying the egg baskets, they started down the path taking carful steps in the dark.

Through the stormy gale and rain that kept showering, they heard a galloping sound that sounded more like thunder coming towards them and the next moment, a man on horseback arrived completely drenched.

Rachel couldn't make out his face, but right now he was the best thing that could have happened to them.

"Bishop, Maryanne sent me to see what was keeping you," he shouted over the raging storm, "What happened to the buggy?"

Rachel took over from the Bishop, while he explained to the stranger exactly what had happened, and suggested that they come to recover the buggy in the morning once the rain has passed.

"Betty, you will have to get on the horse with Amity, Rachel you will walk with Uri and I," the Bishop instructed and then the stranger named Uri, helped Amity, and then Betty on to the horse.

Together they slowly made their way back to society, the first stop was Amity's house, where the Bishop helped to get her inside, and seen to, then it was Rachel's turn and finally Uri, Bishop Gunther and Betty made their way to the Bishop's house.

~*~

After Rachel had changed into her night dress and towel dried her wet hair, she deposited herself in front of the fire place. The night had turned out a complete disaster. She was sure it was punishment for their bad behaviour. Lusting like that over fictitious men and so on. She wrapped her quilt around her shoulders and reached for her bible. She knew better than to let her judgement be influenced by anyone. Despite the guilt, she somehow found her mind drifting to the stranger who came to their aid. She still couldn't see his face clearly, but she was sure he was handsome, and strong.

She shook her head to chase away the thoughts and closed her eyes, and said a silent prayer of repentance. She was never going to look at those magazines again.

Chapter 2

The sun broke through the parted curtains in Rachel's room and she pinched her eyes shut. The night before had taken its toll on her, and resulted in her oversleeping when there was still so much to do. She was yet to feed the geese and get ready to go to the local market to deliver the eggs she had collected the day before, but she simply had no will power.

"Rachel!" Her step-mother called from the kitchen, "Come have your breakfast!"

Rachel covered her eyes with her forearm and sighed. She just needed a few more minutes of sleep, but she knew where her priorities lay. She willed herself out of bed and rushed around the room to get ready for the day. By the time she got to the kitchen her mother had already cleaned the dishes, and Rachel's breakfast was waiting.

"The Bishop and his friend were here earlier," Elsa commented in passing, "Looks like you girls had a rough night."

"Yeah, we got caught in the storm," she mumbled.

So the stranger is one of the Bishop's friends, which means he was old, she thought to herself.

"Apparently Amity had twisted her ankle quite badly, but she will be fine in a few days."

"I figured. She stepped in a hole when she tried to get out of the buggy, we couldn't see much."

Elsa came to sit at the table with her, "You girls need to be more careful, things could have been a lot worse."

Sometimes Rachel couldn't help but wonder what Elsa's agenda really was. At times she treated her like a stranger, barely paying attention to her, and other times she came across all motherly. And all this time Rachel had no choice but to keep her own emotions all bottled up.

"We will," Rachel said and stood up to wash her plate, "I'm taking the eggs to the market, is there anything you need me to do?"

"Oh not to worry about the eggs, I've already sold delivered them this morning."

Rachel felt as if she could crush the plate in her hands. Those eggs were her eggs, her income. She was saving money for herself, and now Elsa had taken the little bit she could earn for herself.

"Thank you," she said tight lipped without turning around.

"I hope you don't mind, your father does need some money to buy that new gas stove so, I figured every penny would help."

"Of course," Rachel turned around this time, with a fake smile plastered on her face, "I'll just get more eggs to get money for my new dress."

"Why on earth would you need a new dress?" Elsa said with mock surprise, "Don't you have enough as it is?"

Rachel was slowly starting to lose her temper, but she fought hard to remain calm, "I only have three dresses, and I need one for church, the others are all worn and faded."

Elsa laughed, "It's not like you'll be catching anyone's eye, and you're past the point of marriage. You're already considered a spinster."

"I'm only twenty-two, the same age my mother married," Rachel protested.

"And see how that turned out."

Elsa had barely said the words when her sons, Caleb and Alfred came into the kitchen, and Rachel had to hide her anger. She simply scooped up her empty egg baskets and stormed out of the house. How that woman dared say such heartless things and get away with it, was beyond her she thought as she marched determinedly in no particular direction. But as the anger subsided, it was replaced by doubt. Maybe it was too late for her to marry, but then the same applied to Betty and Amity, they were both the same age. Obviously living in Derby Creek wasn't much help either, there were far more women than men here, and unless they had gatherings from nearby towns, chances of finding a suitor was slim.

First of all there was Betty, who insisted that she was waiting for Mr Right, she refused to settle for less, then there's Amity who also had her own ideas of a suitor, and the few men that did ask for her hand in the past, were coldly turned down because she was just not interested. Rachel always thought that Amity was the kind who would go on a Rumspringa if her father allowed her, out of the three friends, she was the adventurous one.

Rachel grunted a loud oomph as she collided with someone sending her baskets flying. Thankfully they were empty; otherwise they would both have been covered in egg yolk. She stumbled back and started to apologize profusely when she swallowed her words, and a pair of very strong hands cupped her shoulders.

"Are you alight?" the young man asked, and offered her a lopsided smile.

"Jah, I am fine, I-I wasn't paying attention, I'm sorry," she said struggling to breathe.

"It's quite alright, you were miles away there for a second, I'm Uri, Rachel right?" he said and released her as he tucked his thumbs into his suspenders.

Uri, the name immediately rang a bell. He was Bishop Gunther's friend, but how? He was so young, she wondered.

"How do you know my name?" she asked foolishly.

"I came to your rescue last night in the storm, but I suppose you won't recognise me, it was rather dark."

"Oh! Oh right, yes. Well... um, I'll be going now. Thank you, I mean sorry, I... I have to go."

Rachel just about ran away from him, she had acted like a complete and utter fool, stuttering over her words like a second grader having to do an oral assignment. No wonder she was single. She couldn't sit in the company of a man without feeling awkward. As she hurried away she could feel his eyes burn into the back of her, but she refused to glance back. The farther she got away the quicker her out of control heart and raging butterflies would quieten down.

"Rachel!" It was Betty who waved her down, "Where are you heading?"

"Eggs!"

"You're going to Eggs?" Betty giggled.

"No, ugh, I'm going to collect eggs silly," she corrected herself as Betty fell into step next to her, "How is Amity doing?"

"She's fine, but you look like you've seen a ghost, why are you in such a hurry," Betty said as she tried to keep up to Rachel's pace.

"I need to sell enough eggs to buy a new dress. The cow sold all the eggs I collected yesterday."

"What a cow, did she not even ask you?"

"Does she ever?"

The rest of the way, the two friends walked in silence, Betty on her own planet, and Rachel trying to get Uri out of her mind. She hadn't expected him to be so young, nor did she expect him to know her name. The night before was a bit of a blur with everything going on, and she mostly remembered walking beside Bishop Gunther while Uri guided the horse by its reins with Amity and Betty on horseback.

"Is Uri your..."

"Don't you think Uri is..."

They both said at the same time and then burst out laughing.

"Uri is so handsome," Betty continued, "The last time I saw him was when we were kids. His family has been in Germany for the past few years."

"I didn't expect him to be so young," Rachel said, "Are they staying here?"

"Only Uri, he's staying at our house and is helping papa with a few things."

Rachel could hear by Betty's tone that she was keen on Uri, and she knew by the seam of her dress, that Amity will be just as taken by him.

One of them will most certainly catch his eyes, she thought and smiled softly. Her friends or at least one of them deserved a good strong man to care for them.

She dismissed the notion of Uri straight away, knowing that she would never stand a chance. She could hardly string together a proper sentence when she bumped into him earlier.

Chapter 3

Amity humped along with a crutch in one hand, while Betty excitedly skipped besides them. For the first time in who knows how long, Betty and Amity had made some effort to look presentable, both of them had brand new dresses. It was the Friday night frolic, where most boys got to voice their intentions.

Betty was nervous; as usual she was shy and nervous. She never liked these events much, she did not trust the thing called love, her father loved once, he had promised his her mother that he would make sure she was taken care of, but now years later, all she had to remember her mother by was a single letter, and a lifetime of regret. Elsa was kind in some ways, but she was jealous of Betty, and Betty never did much right in her eyes.

The people from the surrounding farms started to arrive, old and young, in the middle of the big barn the table was set as always. Food in excess was spread across the table, along with lanterns casting a dim glow over everything.

"Have you seen how handsome Uri is?" Betty whispered under her breath.

Amity giggled and shifted in her chair, "I know right? I can still feel his hands on my hips as he helped me on to the horse."

"Oh and weren't they the biggest stronger hands ever?" Betty swooned.

"I'm going to make a play for him you know?" Amity murmured under her breath.

"No you're not, I am, and I've already spent some quality time with him."

Betty wagged her brows and reached for bunch of grapes.

"You can't eat now, we have to say thanks first," Amity said slapping Betty's hand.

"Oh please, no one is even looking."

Betty listened to her friends as they cooed over the newcomer and she opted not to show any interest. They had reason to try and win his affection, she had none. She will see this night through and make the best of a bad situation. Besides, she had a lot more on her mind. Maybe it was time she accepted the fact that she was a spinster, and she figured it was time she spoke to the Bishop and go his take on her moving out of her paternal home into her own. She could always offer her help as a teacher. She knew how to read, in fact she loved reading. She could go spend time at the local school and read to the youngsters, even help the school teachers to give extra lessons in literacy.

"Rachel!" Amity's voice broke into her thoughts.

"Oh... sorry I wasn't listening," she apologised.

"I was saying, maybe all three of us should play for Uri, we can see which one he picks."

Rachel raised her brows, "He's not up for auction, it's a silly game you're wanting to play."

"Stop being such a drab! It will be fun."

No it won't, she thought. The first thing that is bound to happen is that Uri will pick either Betty or Amity, then that will leave one or the other angry and disappointed, ruining a friendship of many years.

"I'm not a drab, I'm just saying. What if he picks Betty, then you'll be angry, not?"

Amity rolled her eyes, "You take things way to seriously, if he picks Betty, then so be it, I'm hardly desperate to marry."

"Come on Rachel, it will be fun; besides, maybe he shows no interest in any of us, then at least we know we all tried."

Betty worried her lip and looked down at her hands, "I don't know, I suppose no harm can come of it." She for one knew that she won't be the least bit phased if he picked Amity or Betty, because she knew she stood no chance.

Amity shoved her elbow into Rachel's ribs and gestured with her head towards the door. Talk of the devil, Uri was heading straight down the path on the opposite side of the table with his eyes fixed on them. And once again the sight of him made her heart race and as she watched him approach it was as if all else around her faded. She had tunnel vision and it was only him looking straight at her. When he finally stopped and took a seat directly opposite her she averted her eyes immediately. Of course, Amity kicked her under the table and Rachel cleared her throat uncomfortably.

"*Hallo* Uri," she said.

"*Hoe gaan het*, Rachel?" he smiled.

She only nodded, her tongue felt like led in her mouth, and her palms were sweaty.

Betty and Amity both fell right into conversation, putting their best foot forward while Rachel wanted nothing but to flee. Soon enough the evening got on the way, with youngsters all frolicking and enjoying the event. Uri made sure he mingled with everyone and never let on that he was interested in any of them in particular, which was funny, since Betty put her best foot forward and out rightly told him he had beautiful eyes.

As the evening drew to a close and most of the people had left, the last remaining few spent the rest of the time talking about the up and coming barn raising event. Uri was still seated across from Rachel, and Betty and Amity had moved closer to where Bishop Gunther was. He was playing the harmonica, which was probably the only instrument allowed in the community, but still sounded like heaven.

"So Rachel, have you always lived here?" Uri asked curiously as he picked on some of the bread sticks on his plate.

"*Jah*, I was born here," she said and offered him a shy smile.

"I'm surprised I don't remember you?"

"I'm not exactly the most memorable of all," she laughed.

"Oh but you are, you are a very beautiful woman."

Rachel blushed profusely and covered the side of her face with her hand, "Thank you," she mumbled.

"Can I pick you up for church on Sunday?"

Shocked at his request, Rachel shifted uncomfortably in her seat and worried her lip, as tempting as it was, she wasn't so sure if it was a good idea. But then again, Betty and Amity did say that they should all try and win his affection. She looked down at her empty plate and smiled. Perhaps it was time she stepped out of her comfort zone and tried dating at least, after all, he was simply going to take her to church, and it wasn't like he was proposing to her at all.

"Sure," she said and then got up, "I have to go now. I will see you around."

She saw his mouth open and close, but she rushed away regardless. She said her goodbyes to her friends and the rest of the community who were all still in the barn and headed home. Her mind was racing and her heart even more. For the life of her she couldn't understand what Uri saw in her. *You're a beautiful woman* – he had said, and it made her feel as if she was about to fly into the night sky on wings of angels. No boy, or man for that matter, had ever paid her such a compliment, and coming from someone as handsome and Uri, made her tummy do strange things.

Chapter 4

Uri was up and ready long before dawn on Sunday, making sure his buggy was clean and that he too was dressed in his best church clothes. He couldn't deny the fact that he felt bad for Betty, she had shown her affection so openly, but there was just no chemistry between them. Unlike Rachel, Betty was just too flamboyant to his liking. She was a pretty woman, but not even nearly as pretty as Rachel. Rachel was unusually pretty, with red hair that always seemed so perfectly plated and rolled up under her prayer cap, with loose strands that tickled her cheeks. The slight dusting of freckles across her nose, that spread to her cheeks made her even prettier, almost innocent not to mention the way she blushed every time he spoke to her.

He was quite surprised when she accepted his request to start off with, but pleased nonetheless.

The first night he saw the shy girl, with her baskets filled with eggs, he was intrigued. She was in control despite the stormy weather and their predicament, and even when he lifted the other two on to the horse, she never uttered as single complaint. She walked quietly next to them as if she was taking a stroll. Not even the rain slanting heavily against them broke through her composure. Maybe it was the way she kept to herself, or the way her eyes lit up the next day when he bumped into her, he wasn't quite sure himself, but if he had to pin it to one thing, it was God's will. It was God's will that he returned to Derby Creek after all these years and God had sent the storm so that he could meet his future wife.

"Uri, you're up early," Betty said as she entered the kitchen where he was having his morning tea.

"Jah, up and ready for church," he said and grinned excitedly.

She came to sit next to him and perched her chin on her hand, looking at him all dreamy eyed. Shifting slightly to get some distance, he smiled and shoved the plate of rusks closer to her.

"I'm on my way to collect Rachel for church," he announced, not sure how Betty would react.

From day one, she had made it no secret that she fancied him; neither did Amity, so it was better if he got it out in the open before either of them got their hopes up.

"Rachel?" Betty said scrunching up her face, "Have you asked her then?"

He nodded and took the last sip of his tea, "Jah, she's a shy one, but she accepted my offer."

Betty scratched her head and slumped back in her chair, and Uri could just imagine what thoughts were flitting through her mind, hoping that this would not ruin their friendship. But when Betty stood up and held her hand up for a high-five, he grinned.

"She's a dear friend, but a nervous wreck, you best make sure you treat her right," Betty grinned, "She's had a lot of hardship with that stepmother of hers."

Uri frowned, tempted to ask about this stepmother, but held back. If anyone was going to tell him about Rachel, it was Rachel herself. He would want for no secrets or tall tales to come from anyone other than her.

He looked at the clock against the wall in the kitchen and took his hat, nodded at Betty and headed out. For a man nearing his thirties, he felt like teenager himself.

~*~

Rachel waited outside for Uri's arrival and her stomach was doing wild flips, while her heart was missing beats every so often trying to keep up the pace. She had never entertained the advances of a man, and had no idea how to behave in the presence of one who had made his intensions clear. A boy simply did not offer a girl a ride in his buggy unless he was interested in her as more than a friend. This was serious business. She also omitted to let her father know, because she knew that Elsa would have a hundred and one things to say about it. She shifted on the swing chair changing her position, trying to find the one that made her feel most at ease, but her body felt awkward. Her arms felt as if they were too long, her legs felt numb and overall her body and mind appeared to be disconnected. Tired of trying to figure out the best seating position she stood up and paced up and down the porch, and then finally she opted for leaning against the pillar. Just in time too, as she heard the nearing rumble of a buggy, which could only have been Uri.

When he came to a stop in front of her gate, she quickly rushed down the stairs.

"Morning Rachel, you look lovely today," Uri said as he climbed out and came around to help her in.

"Good morning," she said softly.

"Did you sleep well?"

"Jah, I did, thank you."

It took her some time to loosen up and say more than four words at a time, but Uri had this amazing ability to make her feel free. With him she didn't have to count every word, or watch her tongue. She could just say what she wanted. On their way to church, he asked her about the things she likes most. The talked about her life, and her family, she didn't feel like she needed to hide anything from him at all. She even admitted how she felt about Elsa, which made her feel less restricted. At church, they didn't sit next to each other, but Betty and Amity were curious as ever.

"So he picked you did he?" Amity whispered under her breath.

"I don't know, maybe," Rachel murmured.

"You're blind as a bat; everyone can see he likes you."

Rachel blushed and kept her head down, her friends were impossible and as much as she tried to pay attention to the service she couldn't. If it wasn't for Betty or Amity, whispering to her under their breaths, it was the sure awareness of Uri watching her. And that did not go unnoticed by her friends either.

By the time the service had come to an end, Rachel couldn't wait to get outside to catch a breath of fresh air, and steal a moment for herself, but it was short lived.

"You never told us you're meeting a boy?" Elsa said as she came to stand next to Rachel.

"I didn't know I needed your permission," Rachel said blankly.

"Well I suppose you are old enough to make your own, but you know, Albert will be very disappointed that you never told him."

Rachel knew exactly what Elsa was playing at, and this time she was not going to let the woman who pretends to care throw any hurdles in her way.

"I think he'll live, and you should be too pleased that I won't be a bother to you for much longer."

Talk about rushing into things, Rachel thought as she hurried away from Elsa, it wasn't as if Uri was going to ask for her hand in marriage, they hardly knew each other. But even if that wasn't the case, whatever happened, come the beginning of winter, she would move out anyway and start her own life, with or without a husband.

Chapter 5

Uri had spent most of the time getting to know Rachel, and the more he got to know her, the more he was convinced that she was the perfect wife for him. He had spent almost every evening visiting with Rachel and in the past few months since they started their courtship he got to know a woman, who despite her adversities in life, rose above it all. Her stepmother no longer tried to boss her around, and her father was too pleased that his only daughter is finally blooming.

It was a perfect autumn day; the ground was covered in a carpet of reds and golds that reminded him of Rachel. He had already asked her father for her hand in marriage, and although it didn't quite follow the custom of dating for an extended period, he saw no reason to wait. They were both adults who were in love and certain of one thing, their own happiness.

As usual he waited patiently for Rachel to exit the house, and like two curious toddlers Amity and Betty was not far away either. They had both come to terms with the fact that he had made his choice, and they were extra supportive of Rachel too. As he whispered a silent prayer for guidance, Rachel made her appearance as if the Lord had answered his prayer. Today was the day he was going to ask her for her hand in person.

"Good morning Uri," she said and her smile lit up his world.

"Morning to you Rachel, you look absolutely radiant today," he complemented her and it earned him an even wider smile.

"I made myself a new dress, do you like it?"

"It's beautiful," he said and held out his hand.

He could already imagine the gasps and giggles coming from the two friends as he struggled to find the right words. He had rehearsed it so well, but now here in the moment, he was at a loss for words.

"Are you alright?" she asked and placed the back of her hand against his cheek, "You look flustered."

Uri cleared his throat and caught her hand, keeping it against his cheek, "I'm fine, but there is something I would like to ask you."

Rachel tilted her head and her hazel eyes sparkled with curiosity as she waited for him to speak.

"Go on!" Betty shouted from across the road!

Uri closed his eyes and smiled, they weren't helping him at all.

"Uri?" Rachel said softly, "What is it?"

He took a deep breath, and then took both her hands in his, "Rachel, I have spoken to your father, and I would be honoured if you would agree to become my wife."

The way Rachel's expression changed from being concerned to completely surprise was priceless. She didn't have to answer him at all, because the way her lips tugged into a wide smile and her eyes filled with tears, he knew she wouldn't turn him down.

Rachel flung her arms around his neck and buried her face in the crook of his neck and whispered, "I thought you'd never ask."

Uri chuckled, "I was hoping you would accept."

"Why would I not?" she said and smiled lovingly up at him.

LONGINGS

Tracing her finger over the cold, gray tombstone, Joanna inhaled deeply and choked back a sob. Kneeling in the pasture of their family's cemetery, she placed a bouquet of daffodils in front of the stone. It all felt like a dream to her. She didn't think she would ever lose her mother. She was her best friend and now that she was gone Joanna felt lost. She spoke softly to the stone just as she would as if her mother were standing beside her. "Hello, Mother. I miss you more each day. I really wish you could have stayed. It's lonely here without you. Everyone is trying to be strong. They want to continue life as it was before, but without you being here, it's impossible. I know you're in a better place and you're not in pain from the illness ravaging your earthly body, but it's still hard. I just don't know what to do now. I have assumed all of your household duties, just as you would have wished, but I find myself feeling increasingly empty. None of this feels right." Before she could finish her conversation, she heard the distinctive sound of horses clopping in the distance. She knew her brothers would be coming to take her back to their small home in the center of their community. They would have finished their errands in town, and she would be needed soon to start preparing supper. Dusk would be upon them soon, and after evening services, a good meal, a nice fire, and sleep would be arriving soon.

Joanna stood up slowly and ran her fingers along the cold stone one more time, giving a weak smile of recognition to her brother, Eli, who trotted up on his prized horse, Petunia. Petunia was a gentle creature and was easily broken. Eli was good to the creature and she respected him as well, she wouldn't ever buck him off, even when they were traveling through thunderstorms or if she ran up on a snake in the tall weeds. They trusted one another. Joanna could say the same about her brother, even though she was the older sibling, they trusted one another and vowed to always protect one another through all of life's trials. Eli looked down from Petunia and frowned. He hated to see his sister suffer so, but as a young man, he knew that for the good of the community he couldn't let his own sorrows show. He had to be strong for his sister now and show nothing but unconditional support. Now was the time for them to come together as a family and keep each other close. That's what his mother would have wanted. "It's good to see you, sister. Are you ready to return to the house?"

Joanna looked up at Eli's eyes and knew that behind the deep brown spheres, there was a touch of sadness that lingered there. He was trying so hard to put on a brave front, but she knew the truth, he wouldn't be the same after their mother's passing either. "Yes. I'm ready to return, Eli. Can I ride with you?"

"Of course. I think Petunia has it in her to walk us both back home along the path." The horse merely whinnied and they both laughed at her response. As they trotted along the path, Joanna's voice turned solemn once again as she asked, "How's father today?"

"He didn't say much at all, he merely got up and went into his study, where he read some scriptures and made some notes for service, then he walked out into the garden and surveyed the crops. It was like a typical day for him it seems."

"I wish he would express himself more."

"Ah, you know how he is Joanna, that's how he always was, stoic and stone-faced."

"Yeah. Maybe one day we'll figure him out."

"Ha! You have jokes, my sister. I seriously have my doubts about that."

They rode back up to the house in relative silence only listening to the sounds of the birds chirping and the echo of Petunia's hooves against the ground. Reaching the house, the pair dismounted and Eli walked Petunia to the barn, taking care to make sure she had plenty of fresh hay and water. Joanna went straight into the house and immediately made her way to the kitchen. In her mind's eye, she could still see her mother standing by the stove, stirring a pot or leaning over to get a knife from the bottom drawer. It was up to her now to make sure the family was fed. She sighed heavily and reached up above the family's ice box to take down a larger pot which hung above it. It was cast iron and the same one that had been used in the family for generations to make hearty stews and soups. That night Joanna decided she would make the family a hearty beef stew. They had some extra meat frozen already in the icebox and she had plenty of canned vegetables from the summer and fall's gardening. She poured some water that had already been carried inside into the large cast iron pot and lit the fire beneath their wood and coal stove. When it came to a full boil she added the meat and vegetables. Her mother had always tried to make her stews last for a few days and made it a point to ensure it was filling as well. Joanna added some corn starch to thicken the broth and proceeded to flavor it with spices. When her father walked into the kitchen, he hung his head, but then looked up and met Joanna's eyes, giving her a slight nod of approval. When the preparations were finished Joanna carried the pot along with some freshly baked bread out to the dining room. The family took their assigned places around the square table. In their mourning period, it was customary to set an extra place at the table for the lost as well, so her mother's chair while empty next to her father, had a place setting and was served some stew as well. It would be her father's task to consume it.

2.

After all was seated, her father spoke. "Good evening my son and daughter. Let us all rejoice and give thanks for what the day hath brought forth. Now is the time we must graciously give thanks for the abundance the Lord hath provided us with and draw close together as a family in our hour of need. I was reading the scriptures this morning and they brought me much comfort. Despite our loss, I trust each of my children to go on living and continue to be upstanding and show true grace. Now let us break bread and honor the fallen."

They all opened their eyes and lifted their heads watching their father who broke the first bit of bread. He then passed the plate to the others who took their portions and set the tray back in the center of the table. Their meal was eaten in silence and no one dared to speak until their simple supper was finished. Their father then looked at each of them and smiled. Tufts of white hair showed his age and he had a natural ruddiness to his skin tone that made him look jovial. He also had lines etched along his forehead left by the many years of being contemplative. One would look at him and assume he was a stern man all of the time, but he had crows feet and smile lines along his eyelids that told another story. While their father was stern and quiet, Joanna could remember a time when they were children he would play their games with them and tell stories which made all of them laugh joyously. He was a man dedicated to worship, but he also was a man who prided himself on the family he had created.

Rising from the table Joanna began to gather the dishes and place them in the kitchen sink, as she crossed into the other room she heard her father say, "Joanna, I'm very pleased with all the progress you have made in the kitchen with meal preparations. Your mother, rest her soul, would be very proud of you." Tears formed in Joanna's eyes and she bit her bottom lip to choke back a sob. Her mother, Abigailbelle, had been gone now for over a month, but the loss still stung. Her entire family was stuck living with the reminders of her being. Joanna still hadn't had the heart to clean out her closet or her sewing room. The elders had planned a town gathering at the end of the month, however, so she thought she would take them then and donate them. After all, she was a practical woman, just like her mother before her, and knew that there was no sense in good pieces of clothing going to waste when someone less fortunate could be using them. She responded to her father when returning to the table for a second trip for the remainder of the dishes.

"Thank you father, I appreciate it. I discover more techniques every day. I feel personal growth is important, don't you?"

"Why, of course it is, Joanna. I've watched you and Eli grow through the years and I'm proud of both of you. I personally feel comforted by the fact that no matter how many times I go to complete a task and fail, I always have another opportunity to give it another try. That's the beauty in salvation and forgiveness. As humans, we all fall short of perfection, but there's always the chance to redeem yourself through prayer and multiple attempts."

Eli cleared his throat and spoke for the first time since they arrived home. "I'm glad for that. I know that there have been many times I felt lost or like I was on the wrong path, but I would pray about it and then something would happen or suddenly change in my life." Joanna listened to the pair talk from the kitchen while washing up the supper dishes and smiled. She loved her father and brother dearly but felt lost. She had no one to talk about her daily affairs with now that her mother had passed. She couldn't tell her father about the gossip she overheard while getting notions for sewing. She couldn't talk to her brother about a certain feeling she had in the pit of her stomach when she watched the baker's son splitting wood while hanging their linens out to dry.

She listened as their conversation continued. Her father spoke in a good-natured tone and there was nothing condescending in his voice as he elaborated on the subject matter with his son. "Eli, do you remember that time you came home crying when you were thirteen or fourteen? It was late in the evening and mid-summer. You had just returned from Mrs. Hollister's barn dance, she was having to raise money for the local town orphanage. You came to me and had tears in your eyes and your lips were swollen and shaking. I'll never forget how dejected you looked."

"Yes, father. I remember that well. I had gone to the dance and got quite upset when I saw Pamela Davison dancing with my friend, James."

"Do you remember what I told you?"

"No, I can't say I can recall, though it must have worked, I haven't harbored feelings for Pamela since that night."

"What I told you then son, was that sometimes we think we know what's best for ourselves, but in the end, it's not us who is ultimately in control of that. Our actions may influence our day to day activities, but it is only through faith we can fulfill our ultimate destiny. Our almighty father wants us to be happy, but sometimes we have to learn a lesson the hard way so we don't pursue other things. Your courtship with Pamela, for example, is one of those things. Do you know what she's doing now?"

"No, father. I haven't a clue."

"She decided to go live among the outsiders. Her life has not been beneficial from it, given my understanding. The last news we received in a letter that she decided to pursue her career as a professional dancer. It turns out that career path led her to work in a nightclub for exotic dancing and she's developed a drug addiction. It's in my best estimation that she will more than likely spend a great deal of her life in prison for drug related crimes or prostitution. So, son, as you can see sometimes our Father doesn't answer our prayers for a reason."

"What if I could have changed her? If she stayed with me, then maybe she would have just lived her life pursuing the path of righteousness."

"Well, I know how susceptible young men are to the wiles of women and their charms. I think that given the choice, you would have left and gone with her and been corrupted by the outside world as well. Outside of our community, there is a temptation to pursue wrongdoing on every corner. No matter what your vice, there is some way to purchase it or attain it there. Never forget that on your travels, Eli."

"I won't Father."

3.

Joanna listened to their conversation while she continued to tidy up the dinner dishes. She knew that her mother would have loved that their father was attempting to socialize with his children, but she also knew that her mother would have played devil advocate in the conversation. She wasn't like most of the other women in the town. She was outspoken and often had heated debates on matters of faith or business with her father, yet they worked to balance each other out very well. Joanna was convinced that when God made her mother, his creation was done purely to spite her father and keep him in line.

She cleaned up the sink and then decided she would go ahead and get the percolator ready for the morning's coffee. She knew that would be the first thing their father would ask for when he woke up in the morning. He often preferred the strong brew first thing, then would go out to complete his chores, foregoing breakfast until their animals had been fed. He always said that if one took care of the animals, they would, in turn, take care of you. He lived by this strict routine day in and day out, with little variation in routine, save for the day he celebrated his wedding anniversary with his wife. On that day, both their father and mother would take a rare trip to town, where they would return with not only small gifts for the children but some goods, that were less costly to purchase such as new blades for the farming equipment. Joanna always dreamed of the outside world as being some type of magical realm where everyone had access to things like running water and life was easy, but as she grew older she realized the outsiders weren't much different than those in her own community. She wasn't allowed to do much traveling into town, but when she did she just noticed that the outsiders seemed to base their own value on their material belongings. This concept just simply didn't exist in her community, everything was shared.

Joanna saw that it was dark now outside and with her chores attended to, she didn't see the point in staying with the menfolk talking around the dinner table. Drying her hands on a dish towel, she decided to go ahead and excuse herself. Walking around the side of the table she approached her father and placed her hand on the side of his chair then leaned over kissing him on the forehead. "I'm going to go ahead and turn in for the evening, father. The nightly chores are all completed."

"Ah, yes, very good little one. My precious daughter. You have sweet dreams and remember that your father and brother are here if you have night terrors."

"Oh, papa. I love you. I haven't had a night terror, though, since I was seven years old."

"Still.. think good thoughts."

"I will. Goodnight. Goodnight Eli."

"Goodnight, sister, remember I love you even in your slumber."

"I will."

Joanna walked to her bedroom and lit the small candle that was on her nightstand, it provided enough light to read by, which is the only thing she enjoyed doing in the evenings to relax. Taking off her bonnet, she sat on the edge of the bed and began undoing the long braids she had in her hair. She preferred to keep it pulled up and away from her face during the course of the day since she was often doing chores. The tresses undid themselves easily and she fluffed hands through it, taking her hairbrush and running it through her long brown locks. After she put on her nightgown and hung her daytime dress back up in her standing closet, she picked up her Bible, seeing the notes she had made in the margins. She had been studying a chapter in Revelations that her father recommended. He felt that it would benefit the family to examine the reasons for death together, so they could make some sense of their mother's unexpected passing. She sighed and remembering her place decided she would finish reading and analyzing the chapter when she arose the following morning. Instead, she picked up the paperback she had borrowed from the town's library. It had a handsome cowboy on the front of it and he appeared in front of a herd of galloping horses. He was holding a blonde woman in his arms and she was swooning. Joanna smiled as the opened the book to the place she left off. It wasn't customary for women in her community to read much at all, but she enjoyed the thoughts of romance and found nothing wrong with dreaming about a handsome cowboy of her own. She finished the chapter and blew out her candle, reclining on her twin bed and closing her eyes sleeping almost immediately.

4.

As the dawn peeked through the clouds, Joanna was awakened by Eli, barging into her bedroom unannounced. He let the door bang on the hinges and had a panicked look on his face, as Joanna pulled the covers up over herself asked, "Why, Eli?! Whatever is the matter?! Is it Father?! Is he okay?!"

"Yes. Oh, Joanna, I'm worried. It's Petunia. She's fallen ill I'm afraid. Can you come out to the barn?"

Breathing out a sigh of relief, Joanna nodded and said, "Of course dear brother. Don't be fearful. The Lord will protect Petunia. Give me a few moments to get decent and I will be out there." Joanna calmly got up from her bed and walked to her closet, taking a few moments to pull her hair back and put on her bonnet then putting on her daytime dress. She pulled the laces tight on her boots and hurried out to the barn where she could see Eli standing by Petunia's stall pacing anxiously. "Thank you for coming out sister. I can't figure out what's wrong with her. She won't respond to my coaxing and she's just lethargic. I've never seen her in this state."

"Calm yourself, Eli. Your panicked state is doing her no good either. Animals can sense your fear." Joanna walked up to the mare who was laying down and looked into Petunia's deep brown eyes. She then placed her hand gently on the creature's forehead. She then stroked the animal's head and back, making soothing sounds, just as her mother would do them when they were sick youngsters. "Yes. You're right to have come to fetch me. She's definitely fallen ill. Let's just hope its a bug. Father has a trip planned to go into town to gather some new ax blades for the fall cutting. I'll go with him and stop by the library and see if I can find a cure in some of the veterinary medicine books they have shelved. Don't worry, brother. We will do what we can for her. Just be fervent in your prayers and there will be a way delivered."

Joanna walked back into the home and began preparing her father's morning coffee. Daylight had just broke and she knew he would be happy to get the day started like normal. When he walked in the kitchen he smiled seeing her standing at the stove as her mother would have, fixing his coffee and preparing breakfast for her brother. Eli always had a voracious appetite She set the steaming mug in front of him and said, "Good morning, Father. I must confess it's already been eventful."

"Oh, really how so?"

"It seems Petunia has fallen ill. I was hoping it would be okay if I went with you while you were in town today to look up some medicine for her at the library."

"I certainly hate to hear that Petunia has taken a turn for the worse. She has been good to our little family. I think that's a wonderful idea darling. God can work miracle cures, but only if we're willing to do a bit of the work as well. After the morning feeding, we will go into town. Be prepared. While I'm purchasing the new blades for the fall wood harvest, you can look into a cure for our Petunia. I bet your brother is worried sick."

"Oh, he is Father. You know he's always been close to the mare."

"We shall do what we can. Thank you for the finely brewed cup of coffee. Now I must get to work, the daylight is already streaming upon us and the chickens will be happy to receive their breakfast."

"Thank you, Father."

Joanna finished making the biscuits and gravy for breakfast then poured them all glasses of freshly squeezed orange juice from the assortment of oranges that they had traded for in town earlier in the summer. She knew their shelf life would be expiring soon and didn't want anything to go to waste. Waste not, want not, her mother always said. She also knew that they all need to keep their strength up because as soon as they got back from town the entire community would gather and chop wood for their collective heat in the winter. After completing her chores and cleaning up the cooking utensils she set the meal on the dining room table and gathered her bag for their trip into town. She made certain she had her city library card and decided to take her paperback with her and exchange it for another as it was nearing completion anyway. Looking around the empty room she sighed. She was worried about her brother, but also she felt a doubt creeping into her soul and a generalized discomfort, wondering if this is how the remainder of her days would be spent, taking care of her father and brother , never knowing the love of a man or having her own family to raise.

Her father and brother came back into the house after feeding the animals and sat down at the table, nodding in appreciation at having their meal already set before them. Eli spoke then, asking to say the morning prayers and included a blessing for his favorite mare as well. They ate the rest of their meal in silence and Joanna immediately went to the sink and began cleaning up the dishes, so she wouldn't have to do both the breakfast and dinner dishes before bed. She also was anticipating having a busy day tending to Petunia upon their return. Her father came and got her when the horses were hitched up to the wagon and her brother helped her climb in beside him. Her father gave his horses a quick pat on the head and they departed on their journey into town.

5.

Arriving in the nearest town, Joanna took in her surroundings as her father hitched up the wagon to the hitching post by the hardware store. She got out of the buggy, amidst the stares of the townspeople. She imagined she looked quite strange to then in her pale blue day dress, with her hair pinned up in a bonnet, while her father was dressed head to toe in all black, complete with his wide-rimmed black hat. His long brown beard wasn't shaved, merely groomed and it did betray his age, as spots of gray could be seen in it when the sun hit it just right. He spoke briefly to his daughter before going inside the store. "Remember daughter, be polite to the townspeople, but do not engage in lengthy conversation unless it pertains to spreading the Gospel. I will be here when you are ready to leave but try to find the information you seek quickly. I suspect this lost time will hurt our productivity later and we won't be able to get as much done as we should. Be careful, Joanna."

Joanna nodded and hugged her father before crossing the street and rounding the block heading to the library. She cast her eyes downward mostly only looking up periodically to dodge obstacles. She opened the doors to the city library and the pleasant librarian smiled and waved at her when she entered. She smiled back and returned the greeting. She liked the librarian, who never questioned her when she came in even as a little girl clutching her mother's skirts. The older clerk would give her lollipops when her mother checked out her religious books and romance novels. Now Joanna was grown and even though she didn't get a lollipop, she still felt those warm feelings when she was in the library. She walked up to the desk and quietly dropped her book on the counter. "I need to return this, and I will be getting another one if I can find the other information I need in time."

"Sure thing, Joanna. Have you been doing okay, since your mother's passing?"

"Oh, yes we have been doing alright, thank you. I'm sorry I was in such a bad state when you saw me last. I am adjusting to this new normal."

"Well, that's good. If you need anything, you let me know as always."

"I will. I will see you when I return."

Joanna then walked off, smiling once more at the clerk. She rounded the corner to the reference desk where there was no clerk, but there was a younger looking man in grease-stained coveralls standing by the finance books, looking bewildered. Joanna watched him pull out a book from the shelf as the rest came tumbling down. She couldn't stifle a small giggle as he fumbled trying to catch them all. He turned around hearing her laughter and she was met with a sheepish smile and the most striking blue eyes she'd ever seen. He took her by surprise as she felt her heart beat faster within her chest and suddenly heat rose to her face as she blushed deeply. Before she could say a word he smiled broadly at her and said, "They don't make these shelves the way they used to do they?"

Joanna giggled once again and said, "No. They certainly don't."

"I don't really know much about this place. I needed a book on taxes, I own my own mechanic shop and I'm doing my own this year to save money for the business. Maybe I should have just paid someone."

"Well, what are you looking for? Maybe I can help."

"A book to tell me how to do it."

Joanna paused for a moment surveying the shelves then reached down to the bottom one, accidently brushing the man's hand as she picked up a hefty volume and placed it in his arms. "Here you go. This will guide you through the process."

"Oh wow. Thank you. I appreciate that ma'am. It's nice to meet you, my name's David."

"I'm Joanna. I'm not from around here, as you can tell."

David took a step toward her, closing the distance, and Joanna felt a certain electricity pass through them. She let the heat rise to her cheeks again and once more looked into his blue eyes. He was in good shape and looked strong from his work. He had blonde hair and was clean shaven. He didn't look like any of the men from their community, but he did seem to possess the same kindness behind his eyes and good spirit. He responded by saying, "I wish you were from around here. I'd hire you to do my taxes."

She chuckled at his joke, then suddenly remembered her purpose. "I really hate to cut on conversation short, David, but I have to get some information then return to my community, my brother's horse is sick and needs medical attention I know nothing of."

"Oh, I'm sorry to hear that. Maybe I can help. I grew up on a ranch."

She couldn't believe her ears. She had wanted a cowboy all of her own. Could it be that her prayers had been answered? He seemed so genuine and caring. She explained the problem with Petunia and David gave her the information she needed to attend to the mare. He reassured her it was nothing major that some tender loving care couldn't fix. He then went on to say that his specialty in life was fixing broken things. Joanna considered the gravity of his statement before turning to leave and decided to do something she would need to ask forgiveness for later.

"You have been so helpful David, could I have your address?"

"Only if I can have yours too."

The pair exchanged addresses and Joanna exited the library, turning around to see David staring at her making her exit. She didn't know what had come over her, but she knew in her heart this man was her destiny.

6.

She exited the library to find her father standing red-faced by the door, checking his pocket watch. She hadn't realized how much time had passed talking with David, she only knew that it felt like they had known each other a lifetime. Feeling the need to apologize she spoke to her father, when they crossed to the buggy, "I'm sorry, father. It took me longer to get the information I needed than what I thought."

He didn't say anything, but merely nodded and coaxed the horses out of the lot and towards the path back to their community. Her father finally spoke when they were close to the halfway point between town and their village. "You know why we caution each other when talking with townspeople? It's not because our religion has restrictions on being social and making friends. In fact, we are encouraged to witness to everyone we possibly can. It's because not all people are righteous, Joanna. Not everyone will have your best interest at heart, and the original evil does find its way into the hearts of men. Some of the people you encounter in the outside world, well let's say the majority of them, only are interested in preying on the weak. It's their life's goal, not helping others or doing good."

Joanna turned her eyes downward again as her father patted her on the leg continuing, "Remember, no matter what happens, Joanna, your family will always support you within the community. We, however, could not help you should you decide to live among the outsiders. You would be shunned and on your own, you know it's our way, there's no changing that." Joanna nodded in acknowledgment, silently rubbing the piece of paper in her pocket which had David's address on it. She knew in her heart, that she needed to see the mysterious cowboy mechanic once again, but didn't like the idea of her father's disapproval. He would never allow such a thing, she felt conflicted and sick at heart the entire way home.

Arriving back at the community they were greeted by Eli, whose worried look had only grown more exasperated during their time away. "Greetings, Father. Greetings, Sister. Did you acquire the knowledge you sought?"

"I did brother. Let's go to the barn and see what we can do."

Together they walked to the barn and checked on Petunia. Joanna took care to follow David's precise instructions and administered a careful mixture of salt brine and water to the mare who greedily lapped it up. It had seemed that she had just gotten a bit dehydrated during their previous days' activities and was feeling under the weather. They monitored her condition throughout the day and it did improve as she eventually got up and started wandering back and forth in her stall, anxious for a trot. In addition to that the new blade purchase, expedited the wood cutting process and the community made short work of the wood pile, stockpiling enough wood to last the entire winter in half the time it normally would. They decided as a community to celebrate their recent accomplishment and give thanks to the Lord, with a feast to be held that upcoming Saturday night.

Joanna spent the night quietly in her room after supper and allowed herself to think of David. She knew beyond a shadow of a doubt that she needed him in her life. She believed, despite her father's warnings that there were good and decency in his soul. No one without a good heart, would have freely given her that information she needed to help her animal. Most of the outsiders would have offered their services and charged a pretty penny for such knowledge. Joanna thought of the feast Saturday and sighed. Did she want to be stuck in the community all her life, eventually marrying a man who had little passion for anything in life? It was then Joanna made her decision. She would slip away during the barn dance on Saturday and go see David.

As the community was abuzz with the festivities at the dance on Saturday night, Joanna excused herself to go back to the house, hugging her brother and her father tightly before exiting, saying she felt ill and needed to call it an early night. Unnoticed by anyone else in the community, she then proceeded down the well-worn path and made her way to town. She made her way to the address David had scrawled on a ripped piece of an envelope from his coveralls and knocked on his door.

David opened the door, rubbing his eyes, apparently awakened by her rapping. He was groggy but smiled broadly in recognition. "Joanna, is that you are am I dreaming?"

"No. You're not dreaming, David. I'm really here." She paused a moment, considering her options. She thought for a moment about what advice her mother would give her in this moment. She thought back to when she was a little girl clutching on to her mother's skirt, frightened by some imaginary threat. She would have said, "Ah, my precious little girl, there is nothing to be afraid of but your own imagination. If you don't give your fear power over you, you can achieve anything you want in this lifetime." Joanna hesitated a moment then said to David all while blushing and smiling, "I came to be with you David, and hopefully one day be your wife."

David took Joanna by the hand and led her over his front stoop, making sure she didn't trip over the door sill on the way in. When he shut the door behind her he pulled her into his arms and kissed her deeply. Joanna felt a joy like none other she had felt in her life, spread through her bones and body. He then looked deeply into her eyes and said, "Well. I'm not the smartest man you will ever know, nor will I ever be the ideal of perfection, but I promise you this Joanna. I am a decent man with a good heart, and I promise to make this life the best we can possibly have together. So, yes. I do want you to stay with me. You're all I've thought about since I met you that day at the library, and you're all I want to think about for the rest of my days." The pair then walked hand in hand into David's modest living room where they sit side by side on the sofa, holding each other until they drifted off peacefully.

AMISH CREEK

The train screeched to a halt and Elaine Sheldon had to brace herself for the onslaught of people trying to squeeze past out. Holding tightly around the handrail, she winced when a rushing man bumped his laptop bag against her hips, and she took a few steps back with the impact.

The man did not stop to apologize and Elaine only heaved a sigh and fixed her stance as the train resumed moving.

It was supposed to be a five-minute walk from the station to her apartment, but tonight, it did not feel like it. Her steps were slow and her shoulders were drooped. The streetlights refused to turn on properly and it flickered repeatedly as she passed by. Elaine sighed at the dreary atmosphere.

Just a week ago, these walks home passed by with a spring in her step, looking forward to the person who was waiting for her to be back, the person she had been going home to for the past six months, the man who welcomed her with a warm hug and a big smile after a tiring day at work—until the other day.

Her eyes felt heavy and the long wait for the elevator was not helping with her mood. She watched as the red arrow went down as minutes passed by until it reached the ground floor. Her ride back up was spent alone. She smiled bitterly. The world must really hate her.

All doors were closed when she alighted at the twelfth floor except for one. For a second, she almost panicked thinking that the opened door was hers, only to realize that it was the empty unit beside hers. Boxes are stacked in front of the door and the sound of a man's groans can be heard as she came closer.

She battled with herself if she should help or not. As the next-door neighbor, she knew she should, as a sign of welcome for the new occupant, but she also knew that the feeling in her chest is heavier than those boxes. She scoffed at her dramatics but looked down at herself.

Her arms were already crying in protest with her handbag and laptop bag and those boxes looked nowhere near light so she forgot being thoughtful for once and unlocked her door. She was about to go inside when a man's voice startled her.

"Hi. Do you live next door?" The man beamed at her but the smile didn't reach his eyes.

Elaine smiled back, a closed-lip one. "And you must be my new neighbor," she offered her hand which the man accepted. "Elaine."

"Ivan. It's nice to meet you," he let go of her hand and gestured at the boxes. "I'll be done in a minute. You don't have to worry about the noises." He smiled again but Elaine can only see a grimace.

"Don't worry, take your time. I would have helped you but—"

Ivan waved his hand no. "No need. You must be tired from work," he observed, noticing the formal attire and the laptop bag hanging on her shoulders. "Go on ahead. Have a good night."

"You too," she returned in a clip tone and sent a brief smile again before going inside. The bang of the door echoed throughout the dark empty unit, reminding Elaine that she had no company anymore, that she had to spend the night alone in her empty apartment.

A tear escaped down her cheeks, which ended with bouts of sobbing for the third consecutive night.

—-

There are things in life that once you get a taste of, you'd never want to let go. And for Elaine, that was her relationship with Christian.

They started dating a little over a year ago, when they met at a mutual friend's party, though neither are close enough to the celebrant and her friends so they ended up chatting the night away. A week later, they found themselves agreeing to date exclusively.

Elaine did not have high hopes with her relationship at the start. Christian seemed to be the happy-go-lucky type of guy who always acted on a whim instead of having plans. She wasn't in too deep yet, so she didn't mind it at all.

But as the months go by and their relationship turned for the better, people around them started to notice—that Christian is changing for the good and it was mainly because of his relationship with Elaine. It flattered the female, she won't deny it. Knowing that she may be one of the reasons why Christian was trying to find a stable job, having the courage to pursue his passion in photography, and planning for his future, made her pleased.

All along, Elaine was expecting that she was included in the plan. It only dawned on her that she was never part of the picture when one day, she got home, expecting the smell of pepperoni and cheese for their usual pizza night, only to find a large bag filled with all of Christian's things that had accumulated in her home. They never agreed to stay together officially but they might as well be for all the days and weekends the male had stayed with her.

At first, she thought he was going for a vacation. She could've accepted it, a six-month out of the country trips to take images of the wonders of nature. What she didn't understand was why he had to break up with her.

They could've made it worked, Elaine believed so. She trusted herself to stay faithful and she put the same amount of trust on Christian. It just so happened that her ex-boyfriend did not believe in long distance relationships. It even hurt more when he said that he's not even sure if he's even coming back. His career was just starting, he said. It could be his one in a lifetime opportunity, he said. All Elaine could do was cry and beg him to at least try, but he was already decided.

And that was it. The end of a year-long relationship in just a snap.

—

The pastor was going through the sermon part and Elaine pinched her forearm to stay focused. They had to work overtime last night and she barely had a wink of sleep before she raced to be on time to the church.

Attending the mass was a weekly thing for Elaine. Christian never accompanied her no matter how much she forced him to and now, she's secretly grateful because at the least, she has this one activity she was used to doing alone.

The pastor's voice resounded against the walls and she snapped back into attention. Someone, a man perhaps judging by the black slacks and the scent, sat beside her. She almost rolled her eyes for the man's tardiness but bit her lips when she realized that she was no better for drifting off instead of listening.

The pastor droned on and she could hear the sound of the piano and the jingle of the tambourine but it faded as her lids became heavier.

By the time she woke up, people were standing up and were walking towards the exit. Elaine jolted in her seat, lifting her head from a sturdy shoulder she was leaning on, cheeks crimsoning due to the embarrassment.

She looked to her right and her eyes widened while the color of her cheeks got redder. "Ivan," she muttered. Of all people to fall asleep on while a mass was ongoing, it had to be her new next-door neighbor.

Ivan chuckled and raised his hand to his lip, which confused Elaine. When it dawned on her, she turned around and wiped the bit of drool that escaped her lips.

Clearing her throat and checking discreetly if there was still drool left, she turned back again to an amused Ivan. At least now, the smile reached his eyes unlike the first time she saw him.

"I'm sorry for falling asleep on you," she pursed her lips. An old lady passing by gave her a stink eye and she refused to shrink on her seat in shame.

Her neighbor saw the gesture and he chuckled. "It's okay. You went home late didn't you?"

"How did you know?" Her eyebrows furrow.

Ivan looked more amused now. "I heard your door. It wasn't exactly hard to when it's the dead hour of the morning," he explained.

Elaine nodded, laughing at herself for thinking of anomalous things such as Ivan being a stalker or a creep. It crossed her mind that it was still strange for him to be awake at such an hour but then that would mean it was also strange for her to have just come home so she didn't bring it up.

"Oh!" She unconsciously glanced over his shoulder and found a tiny, wet mark. Scrambling for tissues, she pulled a handful and wiped at his clothes furiously. "I am so sorry," she apologized repeatedly until Ivan had to hold her hand to stop her.

"It's spit. No big deal. No one's gonna die," he smiled once again. Elaine thought he should smile more often. It brightens up his face. Meanwhile, her face was on fire.

"Can I treat you for coffee then? As sorry and welcome?"

"I'd love to but I have somewhere to be. Maybe next time," he said noncommittally.

"Next time then." She apologized again before racing back home. A loud 'I'm home' is on the tip of her tongue but she stopped herself just in time.

Elaine dragged her feet to the sofa and flopped down unceremoniously with her legs hanging on an arm. Tears cascaded down her temples, which progressed into sobs. Her chest felt tight and her breath was constricted.

Earlier, she prayed to God to give her Christian back. She wished that Christian would change his mind and call her, or at least send her a message, saying sorry and that he wants her back.

She was praying but the pain hurt like hell. She asked God why did this have to happen to her, why she had to feel such pain, why she had to feel hopeful for her future for once, only for it to crumble right in front of her.

It was so unfair. She gave it her all but all she got was nothing.

—-

It had been a month since the breakup and Elaine was faring better. She haven't cried herself to sleep for two weeks now and she even had the energy to go out for a walk. It wasn't much but it was a start. She still thought of her ex-boyfriend from time to time, which was inevitable considering every corner of her apartment reminded her of him, but the pangs were getting less painful. In a way she didn't know how, she was getting by.

It was a Sunday and she was on her way to the church. A friend, Leslie, welcomed her with a hug.

"You're looking great, dear." The shorter female brushed her cheek against Elaine's and Elaine had to chuckle at her affections.

"Hi, how have you been? I haven't seen you here lately?"

Leslie beamed at her in delight. "I went on a vacation with Luis to France. Oh, we have to get some coffee later. I have lots of stories to tell you," she narrated giddily, the smile never wavering off her face.

"How's Christian? Still sleeping I bet?" Leslie chuckled and Elaine's eyes twitched. She swallowed a lump in her throat and an awkward silence passed before her friend realized that something was wrong.

"Hey, what's wrong?"

Elaine cleared her throat and forced a smile. "W-we broke up," she cursed at herself for stuttering. It felt more real every time she had to say it outloud and it doubled the sharp pain that coursed through her.

Leslie looked shocked beyond belief at the news and scrambled to wrap her arms around Elaine again. "I'm so sorry!"

Elaine, who had to fight the tears that were threatening to come out, hugged her back, glad to have someone to comfort her even if it was a month late. "It's okay. It's been a month."

She pulled back and wiped the tears that escaped despite her resistance. "I'm all right," she forced out a smile. Her friend looked at her worriedly but let it go for now. "All right, let's have lunch together okay?" Leslie asked, to which Elaine said yes. It had been a while since she had a meal with another person aside from her co-workers and she welcomed the thought now more than ever.

The mass lasted for a little over an hour and Leslie pulled her to a nearby Italian cafe that served great pasta and gelato. Elaine was grateful for the distraction but she could not help but glance at a table for two at a corner. She mentally sighed and erased the memories in her head.

—-

Elaine was working on a report when a call came. Not expecting anybody, she looked at her phone quizzically, which registered Leslie's name. Leslie rarely contacted her through the phone.

Surprised, she accepted the call and had to brace herself for a joyful Leslie who almost screeched a 'hello.'

"Hey, what's up?" Elaine reclined back on her seat and shut her eyes. She could hear her stomach grumbling only to remember that she didn't eat anything for lunch.

"I know this might be too soon, but it's been two months and it's not too soon right?" She said rapidly and Elaine had to sit up straight again and focus on her words to keep up.

"What exactly might be too soon?"

Leslie paused dramatically. Elaine could almost hear her excitement through the receiver.

"Dating."

"Dating?" Elaine repeated dumbly.

"Yeah, dating. I figure it's about time you meet new people. What do you think?" Elaine processed everything before saying an alarmed 'what' as a reaction.

She sighed before continuing. "Leslie, I know you have the best intentions in mind. But if you still didn't know, I barely have time to meet new people."

"But you have the time," Leslie insisted. "Every Sundays. Don't you always save your Sundays?"

"I do. But that's for church and some me time. I don't feel like going to a party or anything after a mass."

"Exactly. For church. And forget the me time, you have more than enough of that," Leslie paused and apologized for the insensitive remark, which Elaine only waved away. Leslie was just telling the truth.

"What I actually wanted to say is that I know this guy, from the church we go to, who you might be interested to meet," Leslie drawled on. It took a minute before it registered what she was suggesting.

"Are you setting me up on a blind date?" She asked incredulously.

"Uh, yes," her friend admitted sheepishly.

Elaine rubbed a thumb on a temple. "Do I have a say on this?"

"Not really. I already set up the time and date."

"Leslie—!"

"I had to! I know you're gonna say no!"

"Whatever. Just text me the details. I have work to do," Elaine grumbled. She heard a faint 'I love you' before she hung up the phone and she felt a little bad for not saying it back to her dear friend.

—-

That night, Elaine turned and tossed on her bed. She couldn't stop thinking about the blind date and she had bombarded herself with too much questions that only left her more confused and doubtful.

Is it too soon? What if Christian knows about it? What if the guy isn't what she's expecting him to be? But then, what exactly are her expectations?

The fact that he goes to her church is a good point, but the thought that she saw it as a good point gnaws at her guilt. It might be ridiculous but she felt guilty for indirectly saying yes to the blind date. It had been two months but thinking of a possibility of a relationship with anyone other than Christian brought a bad taste to her mouth.

—-

Elaine pushed the glass door open before a waitress assisted her to her seat. A man was already seated at the table, but she could not see his face yet.

A gasp escaped her lips when the waitress stopped and gestured at their table, making the man look up.

"Elaine?" Ivan said, sounding shell-shocked himself.

"You're Leslie's friend?" Elaine asked for good measure. She had not seen her neighbor for weeks now. The last time, they only exchanged brief hellos when they happened to meet while taking out trash.

Ivan stood up and helped her pull her seat back, before returning to his own side.

"And you are Leslie's friend," Ivan jokingly deadpanned. Elaine took her seat and began to chuckle. Ivan, amused by the situation, also began to laugh.

"I guess we'll be having a date today?" He asked with a smile on his face. Elaine hummed in affirmation while smiling from ear to ear.

"How did you meet Leslie?" Elaine asked once their food was served.

"I actually knew Luis first. He was an old friend and he was the one who suggested this place for me to move to," Ivan explained before taking a bite of the grilled chicken.

Elaine took a sip of water before responding. "Why did you move? Was it for your job?"

The question froze Ivan for a second before he relaxed. Elaine bit her tongue for the question which obviously hit a nerve.

"You don't have to answer it if you don't want to," She said softly.

"Sorry," he offered a timid smile.

"It's okay," she smiled before diverting the conversation to a different topic.

It turned out that they have a lot of similar interests than they could have expected. They have the same fascination with the Harry Potter series, the same geeky side when it came to Star Wars, and the same passion when it came to football—though Elaine loved Man U with a passion while Ivan preferred Chelsea.

Hours later, they found themselves laughing comfortably around each other while they walk together home. They stopped when they reached Elaine's door and Ivan kept a good distance, to which Elaine was grateful for.

"I really had a lot of fun," Ivan smiled.

"Me too. I think it's been ages since I've laughed that much," Elaine gushed.

He put his hands in his pant's back pockets and Elaine mentally chuckled.

"We should do this again some other time?" It was more of a question rather than a statement.

Elaine let out a deep breath she didn't know she had been holding and nodded. "Sure."

—-

She threw the frame inside the black plastic bag and flinched at the sound of breaking glass. Next were the t-shirts and boxers that were definitely not hers, followed by other toilet utilities that were never meant for a woman.

It was a day after her blind date and last night, she had the urge to throw away everything that reminded her of Christian. It had been months but she still kept some of his belongings that he left there, silently holding on to the hope that he would come back.

This move did not mean anything but a sign of her trying to move on. She had been meaning to do it for weeks but the date with Ivan was the last push she needed to start working on it. She sniffed and sobbed for the first few minutes but it got better as the plastic bag got fuller.

It was filled with pictures, letters, dried flowers, candy and chocolate wrappers, and almost every single thing that Christian gave her during their relationship, including the bracelet that he gifted to her last Christmas. It took a lot of emotional effort but afterwards, she felt lighter, as if an invisible baggage was thrown away.

The door next to her opened just as she was pulling the plastic bag outside to throw it in the bin. Ivan looked as surprised as she was. He was sporting a shirt paired with loose shorts and running shoes.

"Going for a run at night?" She asked, eyeing his outfit.

Ivan shrugged. "The park's good enough for some laps."

Elaine stopped for a second to think before taking a leap of faith. "Mind if I join you?"

—

The night was a bit chilly but fortunately, there was minimal wind.

Elaine had been living in that neighborhood for years but it was the first time that she jogged at the park. She always thought it was full of rowdy teenagers getting drunk or creeps who had nothing better to do with their lives. Ivan laughed at her when she voiced it out.

"This place's actually good," He panted, arms swinging as they jogged around the vicinity. "You should just avoid Friday nights because it can be too crowded."

She looked at him curiously. "How long have you been going here?" She asked, breaths coming short. Ivan slowed his pace a bit.

"Since the first week I moved," he answers. "It was a bit lonely staying indoors."

Elaine stopped in her tracks, causing Ivan to stop too.

"I am so sorry for being a very unwelcoming neighbor. I should have made you something and came over to check on you."

Ivan rested a hand on her head and ruffled her hair. Elaine felt like pulling away but didn't, surprised at how large his hand felt. "No need to feel sorry. I know it wasn't your best day then," he continued jogging and she followed automatically.

She gulped as she remembered that day. It was definitely one of her most miserable days. "Yeah. My boyfriend just broke up with me a few days before that," she chuckled dryly. This time, it was Ivan who stopped first.

"I am so sorry to hear that."

She pursed her lips in thought. "It's okay. I've been doing great. It wasn't an excuse to not welcome you," she patted his shoulder, signaling him to continue moving.

It was silent for a few minutes before Ivan spoke up again.

"I just got divorced a few months ago."

Elaine screeched to a halt. "What?" Her eyes widen at her rude reaction. "I mean, when?"

"A few weeks before I moved," Ivan looked down. "My ex-wife and I just got divorced and I realized I can't stay at our home for long so I sold it, and moved here," he gestured at his surroundings with feigned enthusiasm. "And I think I made a great decision."

Elaine took a step closer before wrapping her arms around him. "I am sorry to hear that."

She could feel him shaking his head as he hugged her back. "I guess we're both sorry to hear about each other's heartbreaks?" he joked to lighten the mood. She pushed him back and hit him lightly on the chest before laughing.

They both broke into fits of laughter, earning the questioning looks of the passers-by.

—

They continued to contact each other throughout the week. They may be neighbors but Elaine frequently opted to work until late night so they can't really meet much. Leslie called once to check on how the date went and squealed when Elaine responded with a simple 'Thank you' and shouted 'I knew it, I knew it' repeatedly until it burned Elaine's ears.

The following Sunday, Elaine and Ivan agreed to go to the church together, causing Leslie to get excited upon seeing them.

She looked at them knowingly and winked at Elaine, who blushed at her friend's action. Ivan chuckled at the sight but pretended that he did not see it. All of them, including Luis, Leslie's boyfriend, sat side-by-side inside the church.

During the mass, Elaine prayed and asked for guidance, if what she was doing was right or if it was too soon to consider liking a different man. When she opened her eyes and looked at Ivan's direction, she found him to be staring back at her.

She glanced away and fought down the blush that crept on her cheeks.

—

It was a Wednesday night and usually, Elaine would still be at work, doing things that were not really urgent.

When she got home, it was way too early for bedtime and she found herself thinking of the man living in the unit beside hers. Curiously, she laid an ear flat on the surface of the wall to check for any noises. She didn't know why but she wanted to check if Ivan was home.

She could hear a faint sound of music and she thought about it once, twice, and multiple times before deciding to send him a message.

A few minutes later, there were knocks on her door. Elaine, already clad in more comfortable clothes, welcomed the sight of Ivan carrying chips and soda.

"Did you bring any DVDs?" She helped him bring the things to her living room and settled them on the coffee table. Ivan reached for his back and pulled out some cases and handed them to her.

She raised her eyebrows at the choices. "So you're basically suggesting we watch the whole series of Harry Potter?" She looked at him pointedly.

Ivan shrugged before making himself comfortable on the couch. "Pretty much," he grinned.

In the middle of the movie, they found themselves sitting close to each other, shoulders almost bumping. Elaine looked at her side and it was only a few inches away from Ivan's. Unconsciously, she continued to stare until he looked back.

"Like what you see?" he grinned mischievously, earning a smack on his chest.

"Your scar," she started, pertaining to a small scar at the left corner of his lips.

"Ah, they're battle scars," he jested. Her forehead scrunched at the vague answer.

Ivan sighed before reclining fully. "I had a bit of a scuffle last year. I saw my then wife with another man and I confronted them right on the spot. And the rest is history," he smiled but the bitterness was pronounced.

Elaine copied his position and leaned her head on his shoulder. It was a bold move and she was holding her breath if the male would shrug her off. However, Ivan lifted his arm and rested it on her shoulder so she could scoop closer. Elaine let the tension seep out of her body.

"I only have one question," she said after a while.

"What is it?" He closed his eyes, hoping that he could answer it whatever the question was.

"He got it worse right? I mean, you managed to hit his face at least twice? With bruises?"

Ivan burst out laughing. "Yes, yes, I did. I kicked him in the stomach, too. It was pretty satisfying," he answered, still chuckling at the unexpected question.

"Good," She said before placing an arm over his stomach.

They watched the rest of the movies in the same position.

—-

Elaine was typing her report when her boss approached her.

"I read your latest report, about the success rate if the company decides to venture in e-commerce." She waited with bated breath. It was a report she had been working extra hard for.

"And I can say I'm impressed. I sent a copy to the higher-ups and we just have to wait for their comments," he patted her on the shoulder.

Elaine beamed and said thank you.

"You should continue doing what you've been doing recently," he commented, puzzling Elaine.

"I mean, you look happier. Whatever the reason is, continue doing it," he said before turning back to his office.

Elaine could only think of one big change in her life recently. Biting her lips to stop herself from grinning too widely, she smiled at the thought of a man.

—

She was preparing the TV and the player for their usual movie night when Ivan received a call. His expression dimmed and his jaw locked when he saw who was calling but still answered it, walking towards the kitchen for some privacy.

Elaine, though worried, stayed where she was and fiddled with her own phone. She tried to give Ivan the privacy he needed but was surprised when his voice got louder.

"I don't give a fuck about it. I'm deleting your number. Please don't call me anymore."

She could hear the sound of a phone hitting the floor and she scrambled off the sofa to check on him.

Ivan was staring at the broken device and his chest was heaving deeply. Slowly, she walked towards him and reached for his shoulders. He relaxed at the touch and rubbed a hand on his face.

"I'm sorry you have to hear that," he reached for her hand and pulled her closer to him before hugging her waist.

Elaine put her hand on his hair and carded her fingers through the black strands.

"It was my ex-wife," he explained, making Elaine halt her actions for a moment. She only resumed when Ivan nudged her hand with his head. "She was telling me about her wedding in two weeks, and that I'm invited." He laughed bitterly. "She cheated on me and she had the guts to invite me to her wedding."

Elaine, now shaken, fought the tears that are threatening to spill. She can feel the hurt from Ivan's voice and it was affecting her more than it should.

She remained silent, listening to Ivan's breath until he completely relaxed and his breaths evened out.

The silence was deafening until Elaine had the courage to break it. "Do you still love her?"

It was a yes-no question but Ivan didn't respond for the next two seconds, nor even for the next minutes.

Feeling defeated, Elaine pulled herself from his grasp, ignoring his pleas to make her stay. She collected her things from his living room before walking her way outside and into her own unit. Ivan knocked on her door for a few minutes until she said from the other side.

"Please. Stop it. I need some time alone."

The knocks stopped, and a few seconds later, another door was shut.

—-

Just months ago, it was Christian who was the cause of Elaine's sleepless nights. It was him who was the reason why she cried and continuously asked herself of what's wrong with her and why do people find it so hard to love her. It was him who was the reason why she didn't want to wake up to face another day and tempted her to just laze on her bed, feeling as if all the energy had been sucked out from her.

But now, just a few months later, Ivan had been occupying her mind much more than she expected he would.

He is a good man. He's nice, funny, responsible, smart, and even good-looking—a complete catch if she dared say. When she first saw him, all sweaty and panting from carrying heavy boxes, she just saw him as just another attractive man who happened to be her neighbor and nothing else. Admittedly, she even forgot about him until their embarrassing encounter at the church. That was how it was, but because of one date, it turned into something more.

Elaine found herself genuinely enjoying Ivan's company as they spent more time together. It started from scheduled dates and movie nights until they found themselves into a routine of being together every other day, whether it was to just talk, share about their day, or watch movies.

It was a routine that they easily adapted too—they never forced themselves into it nor did they set fixed days and to-do lists whenever they meet. Day by day, Elaine found herself thinking of her ex-boyfriend less, and whenever she did, it was to smile at the memories they shared and never to wallow in the sadness and the gaping hole he made when he left.

As Ivan made her feel light-hearted, carefree and secured, she found herself forgetting about the heartbreaking nights, about the times when she went back to an empty home, and about the thrown away pictures and gifts. With Ivan, she felt that she could try again, that she could, maybe, fall in love again.

But it seemed that Ivan thought otherwise. She could still see how hurt he was when he talked about his ex-wife inviting him to her wedding. She could remember how tightly clenched his fists were and how much he was trembling in anger. It was a sight she never expected to see from the usually composed man.

When she asked that question she wasn't hoping for an absolute no. They were married and she knew that he must have felt so strongly for her to ask for her hand. But at the least, she was expecting something along the lines of 'I'm doing fine' or 'I'm getting over it' and it would have sufficed, for her at least.

If anything, it made her realize how much she was wearing her heart on her sleeve yet again. She wasn't in love with him, not yet at least, but she knew she was on her way. All along, she thought he felt the same, that he was moving forward and trying to forget his past heartbreak, just like her. Elaine thought that a part of him had thought about her in a romantic way, that she might be someone who he can ideally like, but then again, those were just Elaine's assumptions.

The problem with her, as always, were her hopes and baseless assumptions. These always manage to fuck her emotionally—big time. She just never learned.

—

Ivan tried to contact her in the following days but she was resolved on avoiding him for a few days. She was aware that she was being immature but she deemed herself unprepared.

Every day, she recited every line she could say once they managed to talk. She imagined different scenarios and how she would react to them and what she should say. She admitted, most of her though-of situations were bad. She wasn't too hopeful that they would be returning back to the friendly yet flirty camaraderie they had formed.

Elaine was far from being level-headed. When it came to feelings, she was like an open book. She never tried to hide what she was feeling nor did she ever lie about it. So when one day, while standing on the train, hand clasped tightly on the handrail, and a man stood behind her and asked "Will you be my girlfriend?" she broke down in tears and attracted the attention of other commuters.

Among all the scenarios she imagined in her head, this wasn't how it was supposed to be. He wasn't supposed to show out of nowhere and tell her things she has been wishing to hear for weeks in the middle of a crowded train. She tried to stop her tears but the various emotions overwhelmed her.

Ivan had panicked, wiping away her tears furiously with his fingers and then the sleeves of his sweater. He was expecting her to shriek or push him away or to give him the finger, but this wasn't in his imagined reactions.

When the train stopped at the next station, he gently guided Elaine out and continued hushing her. Her cries were now reduced to sobs and Ivan cursed at himself for making her cry.

Once she was calm, she smacked him hardly on his chest, before saying a garbled "Yes."

For a while, Ivan was confused why she said that but broke into a large grin when he realized the implication.

Overjoyed, he grabbed her face with both hands and kissed her, right in the middle of the station, with some bystanders looking away from the scene. The kiss was chaste yet sweet. Their lips glided smoothly against each other and for a while, Ivan was tempted to press harder, which was futile when Elaine pushed him.

"But," Elaine sniffed and shushed him with a finger on his lips. "Explain."

"Could I take you home first? It's starting to get cold," he gestured at her working clothes—a thin blouse and a pencil skirt—and led them outside and hailed a cab.

There was a deafening silence throughout the ride home and their way up in the elevator, but Ivan never let go of her hand the whole time.

He led them to his unit instead of Elaine's and she was about to protest but he insisted.

He pushed her until she was seated on the sofa and he sat beside her as closely as possible. She squirmed in her seat and he gave her some space, rubbing his neck sheepishly.

He reached for her hand and turned his body towards her.

He started with a deep breath before launching to his long narrative. "That night, when you asked me if I still loved her, I was sure that my answer was no," He brought a hand up when he saw that she was about to interrupt him.

He continued once she silently agrees to keep on listening.

"But at the same time, I can't say it. It sounds more real once you say it out loud doesn't it? Am I making any sense?" He chuckled. Meanwhile, Elaine responded that yes, she understands because she felt the same thing with Christian.

"We were a couple since high school, and then through college. Most people called us the ideal couple and were just waiting for us to get married. It was as if there was no other way out of it but to build our own family. So I did ask for her hand in marriage and she said yes." Ivan heaved a deep breath, composing his next words in his mind.

"But as soon as we started living together, something felt...weird. A year later, I realized how used we are to being together. We were so used to seeing each other, to doing things together that it only seemed natural that we got married. I realized that maybe, we took marriage for granted, and it was a hurried decision merely out of obligation because of the people's expectations."

"We started to drift away from each other then. In the back of my mind, I knew she was thinking the same thing. When I saw her with another man, it hurt me—not because I still love her but because I was at least expecting that we wouldn't reach that point where we would hide secrets behind each other's backs—especially a lover at that."

"I saw red and then I found myself furious. I was angry at her but more at myself for letting us be trapped in that situation. When we decided on the divorce, it was heartbreaking but it felt like a burden I never knew I had was lifted from me. It felt liberating." He paused, tightening his hold on Elaine's hand. Elaine returned the gesture, egging him to go on.

"I admit. It still hurts. But not because I still love her but more from the fact that I spent so many years thinking I was happy but realized that I wasn't. It was hard coming to terms with that: that I forced myself to think that everything was alright when it wasn't. And then suddenly, she told me the news that she's getting married and practically screaming at me that she's found her happiness. I'm happy for her. We've been together for so long that I can't even bear thinking of hating her. But then I thought of myself and my sorry state of a coward who can't even ask you to be mine and I was enraged because I felt that it was unfair. I thought that I deserve my own happiness too." His voice trembled then and he blinked repeatedly as his eyes began to get misty.

Elaine knelt beside him and pulled his head to her chest, rubbing his back consolingly at the confession.

"I'm sorry if I hurt you. Because all these just came crashing on me and I suddenly couldn't answer. I didn't know where to start. It felt too much." She felt a wetness on her arm and hugged him more tightly. If she could only take a part of the pain he was feeling, she would do it.

"I'm sorry for assuming the worst, and for not giving you a chance to explain." She muttered, kissing a spot in his head to reassure him that she was there, and she won't be leaving anytime soon.

Ivan retreated and pulled her into his lap, resting his forehead against hers. "I'm sorry for giving you the chance to assume the worst, then. If anything, I just really want to say how much I like you and how much you make me happy." He gave her a peck and kept his lips there, feeling the smile forming on his lips.

"I'm really glad I met you. I'd do anything I could so you could forget him completely."

Elaine shook her head no in protest. "No, Ivan. We will work together so we could heal completely. This is no you helping me, nor me helping you. This is us helping each other," she said, gazing into his eyes lovingly.

He smiled a smile that reached his eyes, the one that Elaine absolutely adored, before replying. "I love the sound of that."

END

AMISH HEARTS AND HOMES
STEPHANIE SWIFT

Ruth smiled as she stood beside the front door of the schoolhouse and watched her students file out one by one with their parents in tow. Another year and another successful Parents Day. She couldn't help but feel proud of herself, especially after spending most of the week tending to every minor catastrophe that threatened to derail the event. Some were under her control, but others, like the impending snow storm, were not.

Ruth leaned to her right and looked out the doorway and upward to the sky. The temperature had dropped considerably since that morning and gray clouds continued streaming in from the west. The snow wasn't due to arrive until the weekend, which gave her and the other residents in her small Amish community only three days to prepare. Thankfully though, it was the last day of school before the two-week Christmas break, and she could breathe a little bit easier, knowing her students would be safe at home with their parents and not traipsing back and forth to school.

"I would bet one of my sweet potato pies that will never happen."

The statement was followed by giggles, and Ruth strained an ear to listen in on the conversation between two of her students' mothers, who were standing near the end of the line. She would recognize Abigail Gandy's voice anywhere, and she was intrigued over what she was betting against one of her pies, which were talked about around their town almost as much as old man Brennan's famous peanut brittle.

"*Yah*, if it does happen, it will be a miracle," Abigail continued. "Time is certainly not on her side."

Hmm...interesting.

"I thought she might have a chance when she dated Amos Wright," the other woman, Naomi Simmons, added. "But he said she was too set in her ways to marry anyone."

Ruth inhaled sharply. Amos Wright had dated only one woman she was aware of and that woman was *her*.

"*Yah*, I suppose she will be an old maid to her dying day," Abigail replied.

The realization they were talking about her made Ruth's blood boil from anger, but worse than that, it embarrassed her. She shouldn't have been surprised, since Abigail and Naomi were two of the worst gossip mongers in town – a fact that hadn't changed since the three of them attended school together many years prior.

Their attempt at whispering was juvenile, at best, and they were so loud she was certain the other parents were overhearing the conversation. As the heat rose to her cheeks, Ruth bit her tongue to keep from lashing out.

Lord, please give me strength and please keep my temper in check.

When the two women finally caught up to her in line, Ruth held her head high and mustered as big a smile as she could manage.

"Ruth, it was so good seeing you," Naomi gushed. "I hope you have a wonderful Christmas holiday."

She returned the sentiment, and when Naomi held out a hand to shake hers. Ruth tried not to squeeze too tightly, although she would've given anything to see the look on her face if she cut off the circulation to her fingers. It would serve her right.

Ruth took a deep breath. *Come on, Lord...teach me to show these women some mercy or I'm going to do something I'll regret.*

No sooner had Ruth let go of Naomi's hand when Abigail was wrapping her arms around her shoulders and pulling her in for a hug. "Have a blessed Christmas, Ruth."

The fact that they were gossiping about her just minutes before their boisterous display of affection left a bad taste in her mouth, and Ruth pushed her away as gently as she could.

"*Denki.* I hope the two of you have a happy Christmas too," she replied.

The two women couldn't leave the schoolhouse fast enough, and as soon as they crossed the threshold, Ruth closed the door and locked it securely behind them. Leaning against it for support, she took another deep breath and fought back the sudden urge to cry.

Old maid.

Unfortunately, it wasn't the first time she'd heard someone refer to her by that phrase. Being thirty years old and unmarried in their community was very uncommon, but it wasn't as if she hadn't tried to find a suitable husband. Perhaps if there weren't such slim pickings amongst the men in her town, she would've had better luck.

Ruth took one last stroll around the room, straightening desks and gathering papers that needed storing until after the Christmas break. Despite the joy that came from celebrating the Savior's birth, she couldn't help but feel a small sense of dread too. The holiday brought along with it a multitude of different emotions, including loneliness, since she had no family to spend it with.

Ruth sat at her desk and mindlessly thumbed through the mail she'd brought from home. She knew she should be on her way, especially with the temperature dropping so quickly, but she just couldn't make herself rush toward a house where there was no one to greet her. At least at school, she felt some semblance of belonging.

A bright yellow envelope addressed from a Keith Avery in California caught her attention. Ruth furrowed a brow. The name wasn't familiar, but she received several pieces of junk mail every week, mostly from people and companies trying to sell her school supplies, so it wasn't uncommon to see a name she didn't recognize. As Ruth tore open the envelope, she was delighted to discover it wasn't junk after all – it was an actual handwritten letter.

Dear Miss Drennan,

Hello. My name is Keith Avery, and I'm an elementary school principal from Pasadena, California. I received word from our mutual friend, Nicole Turner, that you were in search of a new teaching position. We have two Amish children in our private school system, and I would love for you to visit and see if this job might be of interest to you. Enclosed you will find my business card. If you are interested, please contact me by calling the phone number provided on the card so we can discuss the details. I look forward to hearing from you.

Sincerely,

Keith Avery

How strange. Nicole never mentioned anything about a teaching job on Ruth's last visit to Lancaster, where Nicole, the only English woman she referred to as a close friend, operated a high-end clothing store.

Ruth turned the envelope over and a blue business card tumbled out onto her desk. Although she'd never considered leaving town, the invitation couldn't have come at a better time. Ruth picked up the card and twirled it around with her fingers, going over every pro and con she could think of. The thought of flying to California was both terrifying and exciting, since she'd never flown before or stepped across the Pennsylvania state line.

Ruth thought back to the conversation between Abigail and Naomi and her resolve strengthened. Why not? It wasn't as if she had a reason to stay in Lancaster anyway, other than her teaching job, and her assistant, Paige, could take over that position with no problem. There were no close friends or family members to tie her here either.

Ruth tucked the card inside her dress pocket and stood to leave. Perhaps a change of scenery was exactly what she needed, but there was only one way to know for sure. She placed a hand against her chest as the realization made her heart race out of control.

She was going to California.

* * * *

Keith craned his neck for the hundredth time as he waited for Ruth Drennan to make her appearance in the airport waiting room. The small space was filled to overflowing with people waiting for passengers, and Ruth was one of the last to walk through the doorway.

She was the only person in the room wearing a long blue dress and bonnet, so there was no mistaking her.

Keith waved his hand in the air as he struggled to get to her through the mass of people hugging each other. She looked out of place and very frightened, and her "deer in the headlights" expression tugged at his heart.

"Miss Drennan?" he called.

She smiled as he approached her, and he was instantly struck by the way her blue eyes sparkled. Her long blonde hair was tied with a ribbon at the nape of her neck, and she had the most flawless complexion he'd ever seen. Nicole once made a comment about Ruth's "understated beauty", but it wasn't understated at all. She was downright beautiful.

"Please, call me Ruth," she replied, as she held out a hand to greet him. "Are you Keith Avery?"

Her skin was soft to the touch, and he didn't want to let go, but he felt like he should show her some type of identification. He was, after all, a stranger, and the last thing he wanted to do was spook her. Keith pulled his wallet from his back pocket and opened it to reveal his driver's license. She glanced at his picture on it and nodded.

"Thank you for getting here so soon," he remarked. "Nicole has told me some wonderful things about you."

She looked genuinely surprised, and when she blushed, he felt his heart pitter-patter a little more rapidly.

"*Denki*. I'm happy to be here."

After spending most of the night studying a crash course in the Pennsylvania Dutch language, he understood *denki* to mean "thank you", and he smiled as he motioned toward the exit that would lead them to the baggage claim area.

Nudging his way through the throng of people, who were headed in the same direction, while also trying to keep from losing Ruth in the crowd, was quite the task. Christmas music blared from the overhead speakers, and with the holiday less than a week away, the airport was busting as the seams with people arriving to spend the holiday with family and friends.

"I've never seen so many people in one place," she said.

Her eyes were as big as silver dollars as she took in the sights around her, and her sense of wonder and innocence was endearing. It was rare for him to come across someone in his line of work who wasn't loud and overbearing, so her presence was certainly a welcomed change of pace.

"I wish I could tell you it's just because of the holiday, but I'm afraid it's always this way."

She smiled at his remark, and they spent the next few minutes in silence while Keith retrieved her luggage and helped guide her toward the exit that would take them to the parking lot. When they stepped outside, he took a deep breath of fresh air before showing her to his vehicle.

"It's really beautiful here...and a lot warmer than Lancaster."

Keith opened the trunk and placed her bags inside. "Our winters are pretty mild. You'll probably see a lot of palm trees decorated with Christmas lights and ornaments while you're in town."

His comment made her laugh and the soft sound of her laughter made his heart race again. When they got inside the small car, he was suddenly very much aware of how close they were, and he swallowed past the lump in his throat to keep from clamming up.

"Nicole said you were in for some rough weather this weekend. I'm glad you were able to make it out in time."

He put the car in reverse, and he couldn't help but notice the way she gripped the seat. He knew she probably wasn't used to riding in anything other than a horse and buggy, so he went slower than usual and tried not to scare her.

"*Yah*. I am too. It was just starting to snow when I boarded the plane," she replied. "I'm sorry, but I have to ask...how do you and Nicole know each other?"

Keith chuckled as he steered the car out of the parking lot and into the oncoming traffic that would take them east toward the hotel where Ruth would be staying.

"Her husband, Dan, and I went to college together. We were roommates for a couple of years before we graduated. He met Nicole while he was working as a security guard at a fashion show in Los Angeles, and he went with her back to Pennsylvania. We've kept in touch ever since, and I try to visit them at least once or twice a year."

He stole a glance in her direction, and he saw the way she nibbled on her lower lip while he drove. She stared straight ahead and he could tell she was nervous by the way the vein throbbed on the left side of her neck. He was overcome by the urge to reach out and hold her hand, but he shook his head fervently to clear his thoughts.

Stop being stupid, Keith. You just met her.

"Do you want to go straight to the hotel or would you like to visit the school first?" he asked.

That seemed to relax her somewhat. "I would love to see the school, if you don't mind."

Keith nodded and moved over to the far-right lane so he could take the next exit, while Ruth kept her eyes shut tightly the whole time. She gripped the seat so hard her knuckles turned white, but he didn't say anything. She was obviously terrified of the traffic, and he couldn't blame her. If he'd been a stranger to their state, it would've scared the daylights out of him too, so he kept quiet. She didn't open her eyes again until he'd taken the exit onto a two-lane road that was practically deserted.

"I didn't consider until after I mailed the letter that you might not have a way to contact me, but Nicole said you have a...community phone? I believe that's what she called it."

He felt embarrassed asking such a question, but the Amish way of life fascinated him, and he wanted to learn more about it if she would allow him the opportunity. When Ruth smiled at him, he gave her a tentative smile in return.

"We don't have cell phones or landline phones in our homes, but we have one community phone that everyone uses. It's located in the middle of town in a little building called a shanty that keeps it safe from the weather."

She said it so nonchalantly, as if everyone had a phone shanty, and her innocence tugged at his heart once more. She finally let go of the seat and flattened her palms against her legs, and he was happy to see some color had returned to her cheeks. As he pulled into the drive at the school, her face lit up in the biggest grin he'd seen since her arrival.

Keith brought the vehicle to a stop in front of the building, and Ruth leaned forward and stared out the front window. She was speechless at first, but it didn't take long before her excitement took over. "I've never seen such a huge building before. How many children attend school here?"

They got out of the car and Keith locked the doors behind him as they walked over to the sidewalk in front of the building. "This building houses kindergarten through sixth grade, and I believe there are roughly seven-hundred students enrolled. Seventh and eighth grade were moved to the high school building a couple of years ago. It's located about a mile from here."

Her jaw slacked but no words came out. The building was set apart from the other structures around it, including the gymnasium, playground, cafeteria, and the football field across the road from the school. Ruth made a complete circle as she tried to take it all in, while he stood by and enjoyed watching her reaction.

"Are we allowed to go inside?" she asked.

Keith dug through his front pants pockets and removed the set of keys that would unlock the building, and when he opened the door for her and turned on the overhead lights, Ruth gave him a shy smile before entering. When she walked past him, the faint scent of lavender drifted past his nose and made him weak in the knees.

"Could you please remind me what grade I would be teaching?"

It was one thing to try and get used to her stunning beauty, but quite another to get used to her friendliness and down-to-earth personality. The women he usually dealt with were rude and high-maintenance, so being with a soft-spoken woman wasn't something he was familiar with. Keith started walking down the long corridor toward the sixth-grade classrooms, and Ruth fell in step beside him.

"Our sixth-grade English teacher, Mrs. Moore, retired a couple of weeks ago, and we need someone to fill her spot. I'll show you to her classroom. It's at the end of this hallway."

He didn't get in a rush, as he enjoyed watching Ruth admire everything around her. She stopped every so often to peek inside a classroom and her whole face would light up. It was like watching a child open presents on Christmas morning.

"Do you have family back home in Lancaster?" he inquired.

Ruth stuffed her hands inside the front pockets on her dress and for the first time since she stepped off the plane, he detected a bit of sadness in her beautiful blue eyes. He immediately wanted to kick himself for asking such a personal question.

"*Neh*. My parents passed away a few years ago, and I have no brothers or sisters to speak of. The few extended family members I have live in Ohio, and I rarely see them."

Keith didn't know what to say at first. His parents, sister, brother-in-law, and two nieces lived within driving distance of his home, and he couldn't imagine being apart from them. He wanted to ask Ruth if she would be returning home in time for Christmas, but there was something inside him that told him not to. The last thing he wanted to do was make her upset, so he decided from then on to steer clear of subjects dealing with family.

Keith stopped at the last classroom on the right and opened the door to Mrs. Moore's old classroom. Ruth clapped her hands together excitedly as she walked from desk to desk and looked at everything in the room. Thankfully, Mrs. Moore left her decorations, so the classroom was brightly lit in a myriad of assorted colors from the wall decorations to the painted tiles on the floor.

"What a beautiful classroom!" she remarked. "How many children would I be teaching if I accepted the job?"

Keith sat down on top of one of the desks and went over the numbers in his head. "There are four sixth-grade homeroom classes, with at least 25 to 30 children per class, so you would be teaching at least a hundred children each day. They reciprocate between English, math, history, and science classes all day, except when they're in the cafeteria or at recess."

He could see the wheels turning in her head, and he was worried he may have bombarded her with too much information at once, but she didn't seem anxious at all. If anything, she seemed even more thrilled.

"Do you have children attending school here?"

A part of Keith secretly hoped she was asking because she was curious if he was single or married, but he tried not to get his hopes up. He hadn't spent much time with the Amish, but he did know they rarely dated outside their faith.

"No children of my own. Just two nieces – one in first grade and the other in fourth."

Ruth slid into one of the desks and made herself comfortable. "I'm surprised there are Amish children going to school here since our people don't usually settle in California."

Keith joined her, but he didn't try to squeeze his 6'2" frame into one of the small desks. Instead, he leaned against it and crossed his arms over his chest. "There's only one family that I know of. They moved here last year and the parents manage a very successful furniture business. Their twin daughters are in sixth grade."

She nodded and smiled, but she grew quiet for several minutes. Keith could tell she had a lot on her mind by the distant look on her face as she gazed around the room, but he didn't interrupt her train of thought. He knew asking her about the teaching position would be a long shot, but he heard so many good things about her from Nicole, he had to at least give it a shot.

"Did the children have trouble fitting in here?" she asked.

There was a hesitant look in her eyes, and Keith couldn't help but wonder if she was asking the question mainly to try and gauge if *she* would be accepted into the fold or not.

"The girls have done great since day one. The other children love them, and the teachers have a very good relationship with their parents too."

That seemed to lift her spirits and she smiled as she looked around the room one more time before standing. "I guess I have a lot to think about."

Keith stood too, and as they walked out of the room together, he tried not to get his hopes up. The double doors opened at the other end of the hallway, and he was caught off guard when Ruth suddenly grabbed his arm and held on tight. "Who is that?" she whispered.

He tried not to laugh, but it was hard not to. "It's just our janitor, Mr. Owens. He comes every Saturday to mop the floors."

Her cheeks turned a bright shade of red when she looked down and realized she was holding fast to his arm, but she didn't step away as quickly as he figured she would. Her body was soft and warm against his, and for a moment they simply stared at each other. When she finally let go and took a step back, the void he felt was unmistakable.

They walked the hallway in silence until they reached Mr. Owens, who stopped to introduce himself to Ruth. The fear he saw in her eyes just minutes before was replaced by a huge smile as she reached out to shake the old man's hand.

Maybe...just maybe...she would say yes to California after all.

* * * *

Ruth stood on the balcony of her hotel room and sipped a cup of coffee while the sun made its debut in the east. Another day was dawning and she still hadn't given Keith an official answer. He offered to take her on a tour of the county, and they spent most of the previous day traveling the coastline. Each destination left her more amazed than the one before it, but by the end of the day she felt something entirely different.

Guilt.

If her neighbors could see her riding in Keith's car, listening to music on the radio, drinking lemonade and buying lunch from what he referred to as a "food truck", they would be shocked. The interaction between the two of them was perfectly innocent, but she still went to bed feeling ashamed. Keith had acted like a gentleman from the very start, but she would be lying if she said her attraction to him was strictly platonic.

Ruth knew the feeling probably wasn't mutual, but it didn't stop her from daydreaming. Keith Avery was a handsome man, and it wouldn't surprise her one bit if he had a slew of women at his beck and call. They'd had a wonderful time together since she arrived, and the conversation had never flowed more freely between her and another man, but she knew the possibility of them dating was highly unlikely. On the other hand, what did she have to return to in Lancaster? If Keith wasn't in the picture, would she still want to stay in California?

Ruth sighed. The answer was a resounding yes. Everyone she'd been introduced to had welcomed her with open arms, and she could see herself teaching at the school. But did she want to risk being shunned by her community back home if she decided to live among the English?

A knock on the door stirred her from her reverie and Ruth's footsteps – and heart – were heavy as she went to answer it. There were so many decisions that needed to be made, and it was her last day in California. Her time was running out.

Ruth looked through the peephole and her heart flip-flopped inside her chest when she saw Keith standing on the other side of the door. She smoothed her hair down with the palm of her hand and straightened the apron on her dress before turning the knob.

"*Guder mariye*," she called. "I'm sorry. That means 'good morning.'"

Keith laughed. "Good morning to you too. I'm sorry to bother you. I know it's early."

Ruth stood to the side and motioned for him to enter. "I'm usually up by five o'clock, so you're not bothering me at all. Would you like some coffee?"

Keith stuck his hands inside the front pockets of his slacks before walking into the room. "Sure. That would be great. Thank you."

Ruth hesitated. Something about his demeanor was...off. He seemed shy and apprehensive for some strange reason. Perhaps it was just being alone inside the hotel room with her that bothered him. Oddly enough, she wasn't troubled by it at all. She could just imagine the look on Abigail and Naomi's faces if they caught the two of them alone together, and the thought made her giggle.

While she went to the coffee maker to pour him a cup of coffee, Keith walked over to the sliding glass door and stepped out onto the balcony. He looked quite handsome in his dress slacks and blue dress shirt, and the masculine aroma of his cologne filtered through the room and made her sigh contentedly.

Ruth refilled her coffee and cautiously carried the two steaming cups to the balcony. When Keith saw her coming, he took one from her hand and moved over so she could stand beside him. Christmas was only two days away, but you couldn't tell it by the temperature. Not only that but people were walking around in shorts, t-shirts, and sandals.

"I still can't believe Christmas is almost here," she said.

Keith took a sip of his coffee and followed her gaze to the family playing around the hotel swimming pool below them. "I might say the same thing if I was in Lancaster right now. I'd probably freeze to death."

Ruth laughed out loud as she tried to imagine him trudging through the snow. They sipped their coffee in silence for a few minutes, but it was a comfortable quiet that sank in her bones and warmed her soul. She would certainly miss the sunny weather if she decided to return home. It was too bad she couldn't bottle it up and take it with her wherever she went.

"I have something for you," he said.

Ruth's heart raced as Keith removed a small box from his pants pocket.

"It's nothing big. Just a little something to remind you of California in case you decide to go back home to Pennsylvania."

Ruth set her cup on the balcony's brick railing and carefully removed the red ribbon tied to the box. When she opened it, and discovered a California-shaped refrigerator magnet inside, she didn't know whether to laugh or cry.

"Now every time you go to your refrigerator, you'll have a little reminder of your time here, and you won't forget me."

Ruth smiled as she ran her fingertips over the magnet. It was such a sweet, endearing sentiment, and it was also the first gift she'd ever received from a man – besides her father.

"*Denki*, Keith," she replied. "I love the thought behind it, but I could never forget you – even if I tried. That won't happen."

She wasn't lying. No matter what her decision might be, she would always remember her first time in California with a smile – and she certainly wouldn't forget him. From his black hair to his green eyes and muscular build, Keith Avery was impossible to forget.

"So, I'm guessing you've decided to decline the offer?"

There was no mistaking the sadness in his voice, and it gripped her heart and wouldn't let go.

"I haven't made a decision yet. This is a lot harder than I expected it would be."

The sound of children laughing drifted up to the balcony and made Ruth wonder if she would ever be blessed to hear such a beautiful sound in her own home. She and Keith were from two different worlds and there was no one waiting for her at home either. She would lose no matter what she chose to do, and the realization was a bitter pill to swallow.

"Is there anything I can do to make it easier for you?" he asked.

Ruth wished he could. "You've already done so much. You welcomed me here and treated me like family from the very beginning, but if I stay, I will never be able to return to my community, so you can see what I'm up against."

Keith placed his cup on the balcony beside hers and leaned against the sliding glass door.

"Can I ask you something? If you stay here, will that change your faith in God? Will your relationship with Him come to an end?"

Ruth looked down and shuffled her feet against the concrete. "Of course not, but...what if being here changes *me*?"

When Keith moved from his stance by the door and grabbed her hands, the sudden movement caught her off guard. She took a step back, but when she bumped against the railing she realized there was nowhere else to go. His hands were hot and the warmth from them sent a chill up her spine. She couldn't move – couldn't breathe.

"We all face the same choices every day to follow the ways of the world or remain true to who we are. This world won't change you unless you allow it to happen. No one can take your faith from you, Ruth. That's something you will always have...no matter where you live."

He spoke with such passion it was impossible not to feel it, and they stood so close she could see the rapid way his chest rose and fell with each breath. For a long while neither of them spoke, and his gaze was so steady she thought for a moment he might kiss her, which made her even more nervous. When he brought her hands to his lips and gently kissed them both, she thought for certain her heart had stopped beating.

"It's your choice, and I will accept whatever you decide to do," he whispered. "Now...I'll leave you alone so can have some peace and quiet to think."

Ruth sighed.

If only it was that simple.

* * * *

Keith wore a hole in his rug as he paced back and forth inside his living room that afternoon. He'd done everything he could think of to stay busy and take his mind off Ruth, but so far nothing was helping. He figured she would call long before now, but it was nearing six o'clock and all was quiet. Keith picked up his cell phone from the coffee table and checked to make sure he hadn't accidentally set it on silent, but the volume was as high as it could go, so he hadn't missed any calls.

He groaned as he flopped down on the sofa. He always considered himself a strong, independent man, but one tiny Amish woman from Lancaster, Pennsylvania had shown him in just three days how easily it was to bring him to his knees. He felt like a teenager again – waiting on a phone call from the perfect girl that might possibly change his life.

A loud honk outside caught his attention, and Keith scrambled to the foyer, ready to tell whoever it was to go away so he could be alone and continue pining for Ruth's phone call.

Geez. It sounded pathetic even in his head.

Keith flung open the front door, and his heart fell to his feet when he saw Ruth standing on his doorstep. He caught the fading taillights of a yellow taxi retreating down his driveway, which surprised him.

"My first taxi ride," she said. "I bet I won't forget that either. Do they all drive like maniacs?"

He chuckled as he opened the door to let her in. He could just imagine her gripping the backseat of the taxi on the long drive from the hotel to his house.

"Some of them aren't so bad," he replied. "How did you know where to find me?"

As they walked to the living room, Ruth pulled his business card from her dress pocket, and he smiled, having forgotten he'd slipped it inside the envelope along with his letter.

"I was going to call you from the hotel, but the more I thought about it, the more I realized this should be done face-to-face."

The tone of her voice made his spirits wilt. She sounded so serious, and that could only mean one thing – she'd decided to decline the teaching job. He gestured to the sofa, and his feet felt like lead as he tried to make the short walk so he could sit down.

Perhaps she was right. At least, with her coming to his house, they would have the opportunity to say goodbye in person instead of over the phone, which would've felt cold and impersonal.

She sat down beside him and he didn't miss the way she took a couple of deep breaths before speaking.

He swallowed. This was going to be bad.

"I've thought a lot about what you said this morning and you're right. Where I live doesn't determine my faith...I do. I can worship God wherever and whenever I want to...and I want to do that here. Everyone is so nice, and the teaching position is a dream come true. I truly feel like this is meant to be my new home."

Keith had never felt so relieved. He was overcome with the sudden urge to kiss her, but he also didn't want to startle her by rushing, so he kept his place. When Ruth leaned into him and kissed him first, he was completely caught off guard...but in a good way. It was a brief kiss, but he felt the ripple of it from the top of his head to the tips of his toes.

"I'm sorry," she whispered. "I hope I'm not being too forward."

He smiled before returning her kiss. Her lips were so soft, and when he deepened the kiss, he felt her body tremble. When they parted, he noticed her breathing was labored – much like his own.

"I've wanted to do that since the first time I saw you at the airport," he replied. "I apologize if that's being too forward too."

They both laughed.

"Does your school board have rules against the principal dating a teacher?"

Keith kissed her forehead, nose, and then both cheeks before brushing his lips against her mouth. "No," he answered. "But even if they did, I'm sure we could find some way around it...together."

Ruth rested her head against his shoulder and he heard her sigh as he held her close against his body. He couldn't help but smile as he thought about the many things they would be able to experience as a couple now that she had decided to stay.

"Together," she replied, softly. "I like the sound of that."

COTTON SHEETS AND SHUTTERED WINDOWS

Lovina rolled over in her cotton sheets and stared out the window at the sun beaming through the ragged curtains of her bedroom. The light from the morning lit up the interior of her modest room. The cock crowed as she stirred and stepped from the comfort of the warm bed. As her delicate toes touched the floor she winced at the feel of the cool floorboards beneath her feet. She mentally prepared herself for another typical day in the remote Amish community where she was raised. She sat on the edge of her bed and began braiding her long, golden locks. Her hair had never been cut. Once finished she tied a tiny, white bow at the end. Standing up, her hair extended all the way down to her upper thighs.

From the homely bedside table, she grabbed her prayer cap, the white cap made of organza and stiff with starch that she must wear in public. She slipped it over her long, golden braid and stood, making her way over to the wardrobe, barefoot. The floorboards creaked beneath her slender frame. The house in which she lived was in need of much repair, but it was home.

Her dress was bound by the Amish community to which she belonged. She pulled out the calf-length, gray dress, and her white apron to accompany it. She looked the outfit up and down, sighing at the restrictions she had to abide by. Just a little color or a little lace would make it so much more tolerable, but alas it was forbidden.

She slipped the dress over her head, atop the white, cotton undergarments she wore beneath. Her slender arms penetrated the long sleeves at the ends and her delicate fingers stretched out toward the floor. Her blue eyes reflected in the full-length mirror that stood opposite. They ran over her entire frame, assessing the modesty of her attire. Her smooth legs peeked out the bottom of the gown. Her hands just protruded from the sleeves. How she longed for something different. To have somewhat more choice when it came to the little things. But living here her options were overly restricted. With a sigh, she turned away from her dull reflection.

Her stomach growled lightly, alerting her that breakfast time was upon her. Before leaving, she quickly raced to the window and opened it wide, allowing the cool morning air to hit her face. It almost stung as the contrasting wind nipped at her warm skin. She turned on her heels and made her way to the exit of her humble sanctuary, ready to start the day ahead.

Before opening the door she took a deep breath, hearing the faint clip-clop of hooves outside. She felt a tear well up in the corner of her eye, but she willed it to stop. No matter how much she tried, Lovina was overwhelmed with pain with any reminder of her parent's accident. No day since their passing had her parent's death become any easier for Lovina. Each day she was reminded of the terrible accident they had undertaken. As soon as she set eyes on the cart outside, laying rusted and disheveled. Unused for a year. A constant visual scar, sitting in their front yard. Although she knew that her brother, Jacob, shared her pain she would not dare discuss with him.

He had been walking down the street when it occurred. On his way back from the cornfields down the road from their home. Their mother and father waved as they passed, smiling at him. The next thing Jacob knew, he was watching their cart overturn as the horses bucked and bolted, leaving the two bodies trapped beneath the wreckage. Around him, people screamed at the sight, but all he could do was rush over to find his parents laying lifeless in the middle of the dirt road.

Lovina was distraught. She cried for weeks. She took to her room and moped. No one could comfort her. Since then the community had done their best to assist the two orphaned children. They stayed in the family home, but here they could barely make ends meet. Her job as a milkmaid at the dairy farm and his as an apprentice blacksmith left them living pay day to pay day. They relied on handouts from neighbors and friends to feed themselves. Still, Lovina and Jacob vowed to take care of themselves, and that was just what they did. Regardless of if it was against the rules.

One evening, months after the accident, Jacob had an idea. He weighed it up in his mind over and over. He had promised Lovina the day of their parents passing that he would always take care of her. That was just what he intended to do. But not if it meant risking her safety or standing within the community. Finally, he decided that there was no other option for them. The need for financial stability was too great.

"Come out with me tonight," he had asked, his voice trembling with what she felt to be nerves, excitement or worry, she could not distinguish.

"To where?" she had asked, but he would not answer. Lovina was wary at first of her brother's sudden plan. Still, she trusted him and so she followed, through the woods and to the city on the other side.

"Where are we going, Jacob?" she asked on their journey. He turned and held out his hand, signaling her to stop in her tracks. He opened the knapsack he had been holding tightly to his chest since they had left the community. Inside was a range of colorful clothing, the likes of which Lovina had never seen.

"I am taking you to the city," he explained, pulling out a pale pink fitted dress and white heels for his sister. She stared in awe at the strange fabric garments handed to her.

"You need to wear these, otherwise they will know we are not from there," he explained. Entering a modern city in their modest attire would surely give them away as patrons of the well-known Amish district just miles away. Jacob had experienced this prejudice first hand after all.

"I will stand over there. Let me know when you have changed. You can put your clothes in this bag," he gestured to the bag from which he had pulled the new outfit. Then he turned and walked out of sight, giving his sister the privacy to change.

She untied her apron and dropped her dress to the forest floor. She folded them and placed them in the knapsack Jacob had provided. She shivered in the cold night air. Picking up the new dress she pulled it gingerly over her head. It was so tight and firm around her body. She looked down at herself in the odd creation. Quickly she slipped the heels on her feet and called out,

"I think I am ready Jacob!" moments later he emerged from the shadows. He paused, taken aback by his sister's speedy transformation. He took her hand and kicked the knapsack into a large bush beside them.

"Time to go then," he whispered and they were off again through the trees.

When they came out on the other side of the vast wood, Lovina stopped in awe. The lights glistened in the distance as they looked over the high-rise jungle. Jacob had been lucky enough to experience life on the other side. This is where he had been during Rumspringa, but his freedom was short-lived. He promptly returned to the community, overwhelmed by the progression he experienced.

Lovina had not had that luxury. This was her first time in the city, even seeing it from a distance.

"Why are you bringing me here?" she mumbled. Jacob's expression became serious.

"We need money, Lovina. I did not want to worry you with such matters but since our parents passing we have been struggling... more than you know." she had no idea what this had to do with going to the city.

"We can get jobs here. Second jobs, at night. It has been so hard for us Annaliese and I need your help. Please," he begged. But she would do anything for her brother. She took his hand once more and squeezed it kindly.

"Then let's go," she said, excitedly.

Months later and they had been working at the diner quite regularly, almost every night. Lovina darted around in her short, yellow waitressing uniform, serving tables left and right. After her first day, she was amazed at how much money she had made, and just in tips. In the kitchen her brother worked hastily, cleaning dish after dish and piles of cutlery. But neither of them minded the hard work, especially Lovina. She was happy to just be out in the real world.

"Order up!" the chef boomed from the service window. He rang the bell relentlessly to alert her of food being ready to pick up. She scooted over and took it to her waiting customers. Now she had everything down to a fine art.

The sneaking around was getting quite cumbersome, however. Her heart raced each night her and Jacob ventured out, against the communities wishes. That night when she got home she collapsed on the bed and stared up at the ceiling. Exhausted, she wished her life was more simple. Leading her dual existence was taking its toll on her. She was plagued with a lack of sleep and a crippling anxiety. Tossing and turning during her few hours sleep each night. Alas, she had no other choice, for now anyway. She felt a huge debt weighing on her, for her brother. He had taken care of Lovina since their parent's sudden demise. No matter how much she wished she could leave, it was not an option.

One morning as she was walking down the street, Lovina was greeted by an unexpected face.

"Lovina!" a man's voice boomed from behind her. She turned quickly on her heel to see an old friend, one whom she thought had left for good years earlier.

"Jebidiah?" she said, stunned. Her grocery basket fell to the ground with a thud as she ran toward him and wrapped her arms around his broad shoulders. He picked her up around the waist and they held their embrace for several seconds. Even though it had been so long since their last encounter, neither failed to recognize the other.

He dropped her back to the ground and she stepped back slightly to take in the sight of her long lost friend. His hair was styled just as it always had been. His dark brown locks were cut short, a few inches from his scalp. It hung in waves around his face. His skin was tanned and contrasted perfectly with his strong, masculine jawline and muscular figure. His chin was littered with stubble, giving his face a slight shadowing.

Their last meeting had not been so joyous. Jebidiah had been leaving for Rumspringa with her brother Jacob. The three children had grown up as close as they could be, spending endless hours together playing in the cornfields and chasing each other through the streets. Since the age of five, Lovina and Jebidiah had known each other. She saw him as one of her closest friends. Or at least she had before he disappeared.

It had been a cold night, pelting down with rain. They stood there, facing each other. Lovina had been fifteen, Jebidiah sixteen. Not a word was spoken for several minutes between them. Too young to realize the deep feelings that connected them, Jebidiah left with Jacob, to experience the modern world with the rest of the community boys coming of age that year. Lovina had waited for him. She waited up at night and watched for him during the day. But he did not return.

Jacob came back weeks later with a few of the neighborhood boys, but Jebidiah was not among them.

Her brother had rested his hand on her shoulder as tears rolled down her face, tears for the loss of her best friend.

"He said to tell you he will see you again. He promised." at the time Lovina had not believed him. She had thought her brother was trying desperately to bring her out of her deepening hole of overwhelming sadness. But with Jebidiah standing before her, Jacob's words echoed in the midst of her thoughts.

'He promised.'

She had given up hope of seeing him again, yet here he stood, in the flesh.

Jebidiah was speechless. He had returned to the community after years. It seemed that no matter how much the modern world drew him, his love for Lovina was stronger. From the day he had left, he did not stop thinking about her, not for a moment. It had been fun and he savored the new experiences put forth by his peers in the city, but no one could replace her. That was what influenced him to return. There was nothing more he could gain from the city, he was looking to start a family. Jebidiah could not consider anyone else he would rather make a life with than her.

"I hope Jacob gave you my message all those years ago," he said, smiling down at her from above.

"He did," she replied, mirroring the beam that had taken over Jebidiah's face. Any onlooker could tell that these two were much more than just friends, even if they had not yet admitted it to themselves. They still grasped the hands of each other as they chatted for a few minutes about shared memories from the past.

Jebidiah bent down and picked up the discarded basket of groceries Lovina had dropped in her shock at his appearance.

"Let's go for a walk, I need to catch up with you. So much has happened in the last few years I am sure," he laughed. As they strolled along they spoke at length about their experiences. Everything Jebidiah said about his time away absolutely intrigued her. She desperately wished that she could share in this modern world, if only for a day. Working was all she had ever had the chance to do when her and Jacob managed to escape for their night shifts.

"So, what about your life, Lovina?" he questioned. After a moment of thought, he saw her face drop. The only significant thing she could think of to tell him was of her parent's sudden demise the previous fall.

She took a deep breath and prepared herself for the retelling of the most painful memory she possessed.

"Actually, there was an accident last year," she began. Jebidiah's permanent grin faded almost immediately.

"My parents cart overturned. It was terrifying but the worst was that they did not make it." Jebidiah could not find the words to express his condolences. After a few moments to comprehend the brief and saddening story he mustered,

"I am so sorry, Lovina."

As always, her first thought was to change the subject, and so she did. Long ago she had decided that her parents would not have wanted her to mourn, but cherish the life that she had. That was exactly what she intended to do. The sadness they had been wallowing in for that brief moment evaporated quickly as they moved on to more trivial and light-hearted news from their vast time apart.

Jebidiah walked her all the way back to her door. He handed back the basket as she stepped through the threshold of the dark, polished doorway.

"Well, I am sure we will see each other again soon," he said as he turned to leave.

"You will," she smiled and with that the door clicked shut behind her.

As the following months flew by, Lovina found herself spending more and more of her limited free time with her long lost friend. Jebidiah found comfort in their closeness. Since moving back, he had faced endless scrutiny from the older members of the place he called home. They frowned upon him for his rash decision to leave, now that he had returned. He had known upon his abrupt return to his family that not everyone would be so welcoming. But no one else mattered as long as Lovina was by his side.

She found comfort in his company too. She was intrigued by his endless stories of the new technologies and strange architecture he had encountered in his years away. Unlike her peers, Lovina held nothing against him for leaving, if anything she wished that she could do the same.

The two companions spent their time just as they did, years earlier. Exploring the now familiar woods. Chasing each other through the cornfields. Collapsing with laughter on the dirt floor of the outdoors. They savored each moment they spent in each others company. To Lovina, no one could compare to Jebidiah.

One sunny afternoon, they fell into each other's arms in the dewy grass of the outskirts of the boundary. Their laughter subsided and Lovina looked up at Jebidiah, beaming down at her. She knew that there was something deeper. This was not just another friendship, he meant so much more. Every second without him left her feeling cold and empty. Every second without her made him feel as if he was completely alone.

"Do you think you will stay here this time?" Lovina asked. She hoped that his answer reflected the way that she felt. But alas, he uttered the answer she did not want to hear.

"No. I think that now I have experienced what is out there, lived my life outside the confines of the community, I don't want to leave again." her heart dropped. There was nothing in the world she wished for more than to go, but a life without Jebidiah seemed just as empty.

It was his strength that encouraged her to plan her escape, to a new life in the modern world. Deep in her heart she knew that it was unlikely Jebidiah would come with her. After all, he had returned not weeks ago, but she had to follow her dreams. She had but one life, and she intended to live it. As much as she wanted to share with him her wishes, she knew this was one secret she must keep to herself.

Jebidiah walked her home again that day, as he often did of late. The sun was setting over the sovereign hills as they strolled past people and places on the way home. She took in the sights, for in a few weeks they would be gone forever. There was no doubt she would miss this place, but most of all she would miss him. She cherished the time they had together, though short lived.

They arrived at her home. Before she opened the door, Jebidiah grasped her wrist tightly. Her skin broke out in goosebumps all over in response to his flesh against hers. Her heart raced within her chest cavity. Cheeks began to glow red as the blood from her pounding heart rushed to her face. She hoped that Jebidiah did not see the intense reaction she gave from his touch.

"Do you have plans for tomorrow?" he questioned. His expression was serious all of a sudden.

"No," Lovina responded. Where was he going with this?

"I see, well goodnight then," he said with a grin. How strange. With that Jebidiah let go of her arm and placed his hands into his pockets.

"Goodbye," she called to him as he strolled slowly away, toward his family home at the end of the road.

As she closed the door behind her Lovina leaned her back against the rough wood and closed her eyes. The overwhelming sensation of lust she felt for Jebidiah was quickly blooming into a raging passion. Love. Little did she know that he felt it too. From the top of her head to the far tips of her toes her entire being was filled with admiration and desire for him. How would she tell him that she was going to leave the town? Start a new life in the place that he had run from.

She already had a plan in place. Two weeks from now she would be living amongst the modern world. Jacob had not been pleased, but he knew that he could not stop his sister from following her dreams. He had the opportunity, so there was no way that he could deny her that right, regardless of the community law.

"Are you sure you will be OK on your own?" Jacob could not hide the worried tone of his voice. Not even he could brave the new world, how could his little sister live there alone?

"I will, please do not worry about me, Jacob," then she explained her plan.

In the dead of night, while the town slept, she would sneak silently through the streets. Toward the wood. The path that they had traveled hundreds of times before would lead her to her new existence. She could not leave during the day, for fear of what scrutiny she may face from the others in the town. Women rarely left and were never welcomed home. It was best for her to just disappear.

"But you have never been that way alone." he said, his voice still trembling with fear for Lovina.

"I have mapped out our way. The last few weeks I have made a note of each landmark along the path. Each time I feel as if my feet lead me more and more. I step without hesitation." slowly she had memorized the way. Every rock and tree, branch and shrub. The dirt clearings and the overgrown mangling of tangled weeds, she was confident in her navigational ability. Even if Jacob was not so.

"Where will you stay?" his questions kept coming. But Lovina was not one to take her decisions lightly. To his every question, she had the perfect answer. During their time at the diner, they had made a few friends, both co-workers, and customers. Lovina had organized a room in a modest apartment with Katie, a fellow waitress at a neighboring restaurant. For only a small portion of her minimum wage, she had a place to her her own.

Several hours later, Lovina had assured her brother that she could fend for herself. If she ever needed him, he would be there for her too.

Jacob took her hand and looked at her, eyes full of sadness.

"I will always be here for you, sister," a single tear rolled down his cheek, winding its way through the stubble on his strong chin. Lovina was taken aback, she had not seen her brother so emotional since their parents passing. She whispered the only words that came to mind in response to his heartfelt confession.

"I know," tears now flowed freely down their faces. They sat in silence as Jacob took in the news she had revealed to him. The plan she had derived. How much he would miss her.

The hardest part was over. Lovina had dreaded telling her brother about her escape. Now she felt free, with his blessing she could leave without hesitation. She slept that night, soundly for the first time in many moons. Dreaming of the future adventures she would have in the big city.

The next morning Jebidiah was at her door before either of the siblings had risen. She heard the light tapping from her bedroom and quickly dressed to see who was so desperate to see them this day. She raced down the creaking steps and to the front door. Opening it widely she was ecstatic to see Jebidiah standing there with a bouquet of red roses. Their scent was swept immediately into her nostrils and she closed her eyes as the aroma intoxicated her.

"Good morning, Lovina," Jebidiah greeted her, placing the stunning bunch into her hands.

"Hello," she replied, staring at the gift he had brought for her. Something was different about him this morning. She could not pick it but his smile was strange somehow, brighter than she had seen before. His eyes sparkled in the morning light. Her heart skipped a beat as they paused for a moment, looking deeply into each other's eyes.

"I have a day planned for us," he said excitedly. Before she had time to properly lace up her boots, Jebidiah took her hand and whisked her away from her home. They walked together toward the vast cornfields at the end of the street. Waving at their fellow community members as they passed, Jebidiah led Lovina through the tall corn stalks.

She had no idea what he had in store. They rushed forward in silence. Lovina found her mind wandering as she took in the rays of sunlight winding through the stalks and leaves surrounding them. Her dress occasionally caught on rouge sticks and branches strewn throughout the fields. She stumbled a few times, but Jebidiah was there to catch her and help her find her feet once more.

Minutes passed and they finally arrived at the small clearing in the far end of the fields. Jebidiah let her hand drop and pulled a blanket from the backpack he had been lugging with them on the short journey. He laid it delicately out on the ground, straightening the edges and patting it down flat.

"Come, sit," he gestured to a soft spot on the blanket and she slowly approached, sitting down carefully, holding her dress flat against her thighs as she lowered her body to the ground. She watched on as Jebidiah began unpacking a picnic that he had prepared. She was stunned at the romantic setting that he had created for just the two of them, out of nowhere.

"I hope you're hungry," he laughed. Her eyes drifted from plate to plate, each piled high with sandwiches and cakes, fruit and salads. She could not believe what she saw before her. This was the kind of thing she had always dreamed of but had never eventuated into a reality. The sun beamed down on them as they began their conversations.

"Please," Jebidiah picked up a plate of her favorite sandwiches, fresh strawberry jam. She picked up one and took a bite. The sweetness of the jam found every corner of her tongue, leaving a lasting sensation in her mouth as she swallowed. He watched her intently, looking as if something was weighing heavily on his mind. Lovina looked into his deep, brown eyes. She felt herself smile as she took in his handsome features, just inches from her. His short, dark hair flowed subtly in the mild breeze. Her gaze followed his masculine jawline and rugged chin, covered in light stubble.

It was at that moment Jebidiah uttered the words she had been longing for him to say for so long,

"I love you, Lovina, I always have." she was taken aback. Of course, her heart reciprocated his feelings, but she could not bring herself to say the words back. In the back of her mind, she knew that if she revealed her love for him she must also let him in on the fact she was planning to leave. Leave him and everything else behind. Moments later she found her voice once more,

"I love you too."

They spoke for hours after Jebidiah's unexpected, but heartfelt, confession. Of life and the paths they wanted to take in the future. That was when troubles arose.

"I just want to settle down, and have a family. I love it so much here. It feels so right to be back." Jebidiah said in between bites of his rosy red apple. Lovina froze. This was exactly the life she was running from. It was the first time that she realized that their journeys may lead them in different directions. She sat silent for a moment as he waited patiently for her to say something, anything. She took a deep breath and proceeded to reveal her underlying plan to Jebidiah. Her plan to leave and start a new life in the city he had fled from.

"I had no idea," Jebidiah gasped, in response to her and Jacob's secret second existence outside of the community. His heart dropped as she continued to explain her plans to escape and live amongst the modern world. Never had he thought coming into the fields with her that morning that she would drop this bombshell upon him. All hopes of his quiet life back at home with his childhood sweetheart were slowly evaporating before his eyes.

"When do you plan to leave?" he questioned, his heartbeat pounding in his chest. He prayed that it was not soon. That he would have time to change her mind.

"Two weeks from today," she admitted. His smile had faded, and hers with it. She had thought that the hardest conversation before her departure was over, but she had not counted on Jebidiah's romantic notions. His proposal of a simple, family life in the mundane town she had always lived. She loved him deeply, but her want for adventure was overwhelming.

With the sun beginning to lower over the tips of the corn, they decided that it was time to return. She folded the blanket as Jebidiah picked up the empty plates that surrounded them in the clearing. He took her hand and led the way back through the towering stalks. They moved at a much slower pace upon their return. Lovina could not be sure, maybe it was due to the dimming light, but she felt as if their lagging pace was a bi-product of the conversations they had just had. Of her leaving him and the rest of her life behind.

Eventually, they reached her front door once more. She stepped up the front stair and peered down at him.

"Thank you for today, Jebidiah. I had an amazing time. I really appreciate all that you have done for me," Lovina checked quickly for onlookers and before a word could escape his lips she kissed him tenderly on the cheek. By the time Jebidiah realized what had happened she had already stepped back inside.

He began his journey home, filled with mixed emotions from the day just passed. He desperately wanted Lovina to stay, but he understood her position was difficult. With constant reminders daily of her parent's death, he could only imagine the heartache she must feel living here.

Two weeks later, the grandfather clock below the stairs began chiming midnight. Lovina knew this was her chance to make her escape quietly, without fear of waking her sleeping neighborhood. She tiptoed down the stairs, their echoing creaks masked by the gongs of the great timekeeper. Her blonde locks fell over her face as she looked down toward the door, her destination on this dark winter night. She brushed them aside and kept moving. Grabbing the already assembled knapsack from its hiding spot, she slipped her pale pink coat over her slender shoulders and on the final stroke of midnight the door clicked shut behind her.

The cool wind bit at her exposed flesh as she crept through the dead of night. She knew that by leaving she was breaking her oath to the Church, but the call of the outside world was just too great. Not even her one true love could keep her from following her dreams. A single tear rolled slowly down her pale cheek as she looked back, back at the friends and family she would no longer see. Back at Jebidiah.

Tearing her gaze away she strove forward. Her hair was now wet with sweat, despite the cold air that stung her face and pierced her lungs. She ran, as fast as she could. Each snapping twig made her heart jump. Every sound around her made her pause for a moment. A moment was all she could spare. Slowly she kept moving, through the woods, following the hidden road to freedom. As she made her way Lovina found her mind wandering back to all of her most cherished memories with the community and everything she was giving up. The celebrations and family dinners. Just as she lost herself completely in her thoughts a sharp noise snapped her back to reality.

She looked around desperately for somewhere to hide. She could distinguish faint footsteps coming her way. Who could be out here this late, in the cold? Lovina was convinced that she was caught. Someone had overheard her speaking of her plan to Jebidiah, or worse he had outed her himself. She threw her knapsack into a large bush to her left and jumped behind. As she crouched on the ground crazy accusations filled her head, but she kept her blue eyes focused on the clearing before her. Was it Jebidiah who let slip her secret plan, or did someone else overhear? When a shadowy figure finally caught her eye in the woods, she waited with baited breath to identify her stalker.

Branches crunched beneath his feet as the man emerged into the grassy clearing, uncloaked by the light of the moon. Lovina's jaw dropped and her heart raced at what felt like a thousand beats a second. She no longer needed to hide, she no longer had any fear or doubt about the path that she had chosen.

"Jebidiah!" she exclaimed, sprinting as fast as her legs could carry her toward him. A smile exploded across his face as she jumped carelessly into his outstretched arms. Jebidiah wrapped his muscular arms around her. He grasped her as tight as he could, never wanting to part again. She let her body melt into his. There they stood, nestled in each other's arms for several moments before severing their sensual embrace.

"I could not let you go, Lovina. I love you." Jebidiah confessed. She stared into his beaming blue eyes, looking down upon her. There was only one thing that she could respond.

"I love you too," she answered. Her eyes welled up with blissful tears that soon began running, one by one, down her soft cheeks. Jebidiah reached forward and wiped them away with his calloused hands. One of her arms drew back, reaching up to run her fingers through his mess of tangled hair, damp with sweat. Still stunned by his sudden appearance, she was nothing but ecstatic to see him.

At that moment, Jebidiah leaned down and kissed her soft, cherry lips for the first time, basking in the cool blanket of moonlight penetrating the canopy. Lovina could not believe her luck as she stood in the middle of the trees, in the arms of her love. She had been sure, not hours ago, that she had lost the love of her life forever. Now, she was on her way to making a new life for herself, in a new world, with the man of her dreams.

She leaned in closer to his warm silhouette, grasping at the fabric of his coat. She savored his touch, something she thought she had lost forever in the sands of time. His hand brushed her now flushing cheeks. He traced down her neck and over her petite shoulder. Her hand found its place against his pounding chest. And hers against his.

Jebidiah brushed a lock of hair from Lovina's ear.

"We must go now," he whispered softly to her. Stepping back from him, she nodded in agreement. She would no longer need to start her new life alone, they were together at last. He picked up her knapsack and hauled it onto his back.

"Come," he ushered Lovina back onto her path. Toward the city for the last time. As they neared the bustling hub, she witnessed the blanket of light illuminating the town. Never had she seen something so beautiful. Never had she felt so free.